Cracks in the Ice

Deanna Klingel

Cracks in the Ice

© 2012 Deanna Klingel

ISBN-13: 978-1-938092-23-7
ISBN-10: 1938092236

Published by Write Integrity Press, 130 Prominence Point Pkwy. #130-330, Canton, GA 30114. www.WriteIntegrity.com.

Printed in the United States of America.

PART ONE

GINA

To Ryan —

Smooth skating

Deanna K. Klingel

Chapter One

Dear Diary,

All I want is to be in charge of my own life and ice skate. Is that so much to ask? I mean I am fourteen. I think I can be in charge of something. It just isn't fair. All I want to do is ice skate. Sometimes things happen that have nothing to do with me, but they change things in my life. I don't think that's fair. Now, I have all these other things I have to deal with. It makes me mad.

Gina, 1954

I like to stand up here, look out my window, think about things, and watch the Dobermans running around in their yard. When I was little I was afraid of the Dobermans. Bugsy, their handler, told me they'd eat me alive and I was never allowed to go into their compound. That meant just about anywhere outside on the family compound.

From up here in my room I can see the play yard Uncle Giovanni's business associates built for me when I was small. It's made of stone and tile and it has a fountain with a spray and a big shade tree. They built a playhouse inside the tile enclosure to look like a miniature of the big house. I liked it okay, but I always wished it had grass. The Dobermans have the grass.

I spent a lot of time in that little playhouse when I was younger. I played with my Sonje Henie paper dolls and read *Little Women* and *Nancy Drew*. I sucked on frozen Kool-Aid squares in the summer and sipped hot Ovaltine from my red plaid thermos in the winter. My playhouse had a table and two red chairs. I never knew who was supposed to sit in the second chair.

I used to peep through a chipped hole in the tile wall and watch the Dobermans running in the grass. In winter they had the best snow. The sprawling lawns of the family compound stretched out from the big house like bleached linen tablecloths. But in my play yard the snow piled against the walls. I could make snow angels, but I couldn't run anywhere or roll around like the Dobermans.

If someone didn't know better, they'd think they were just playful, happy, pets. They're actually working. Their job is to keep people from coming into the Giovanni Family Compound. Whenever someone comes, the dogs go tearing to the gate barking viciously, hackles up, snarling through their bared teeth, and slobbering all over themselves. Now, that's funny!

Then Bugsy picks up his gun that he nicknamed Chicago Piano, and he looks out the guard house window. If it's someone who has an appointment, he blows his silent whistle, the dogs go back to the guard house, and the gate opens. If they don't have an appointment, Bugsy tells them they have five seconds to turn around and get off the property in one piece.

The Dobermans help them make up their minds. That's their job.

Everyone has a job here. Everyone except me, that is. I just live here. I'm Gina, the niece of Don Salvatore Giovanni. I don't play in my playhouse anymore. I mostly look out the window when I'm home, which I rarely am. Most of the time, now, I'm on the ice.

Three things happened when I was younger that changed everything for me. The first was the Dobermans. One winter day the dark Michigan sky was weighted down with a blizzard we all knew was coming. Once it got started, I'd be in for several boring days. The tutors wouldn't come, there would be no school over the garage, and it would just be me and my Sonje Henie paper dolls. I thought the Dobermans would feel lonely too, with no one to keep out.

I waited in the hall outside Uncle G's office for Bugsy to come out of a family meeting. I told him, in a nice way of course, very respectful, I thought the Dobermans might be feeling bored and lonely and maybe needed someone to play with.

Bugsy laughed real loud and slapped my head, playful like, accidentally shoving me into the wall. In his broken Sicilian-Italian-English he told me that his boys, Veloce and Capu, would eat me alive. He'd trained them to guard the Family Compound, not play tea party with a little girl.

"But I'm family," I whined. "You could train them to like

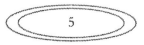

me." I was scared, but even scared is better than bored and lonely. Bugsy always gave in to me when I whined.

We started with Veloce. Bugsy said I'd be Veloce's grocer. I learned to bring his groceries – his meat. It took a few weeks, and Bugsy said it had to be our secret. If anything went wrong he'd deny being a part of it. He said Uncle Giovanni would ice him. I giggled thinking that Uncle G would drop snowballs down Bugsy's shirt.

Bugsy said, "Ain't funny, Gina."

"Yes, it is," I giggled.

By the time my eighth birthday rolled around, Veloce, Capu, and I were pretty good friends. Their names mean Fast and Boss. I wasn't ever allowed to enter their compound alone, but I learned to pet them, give them meat, and tell them to lie down. Bugsy taught me the tricks to training them. I wasn't afraid of them anymore.

Bugsy said a Doberman's like everything else in life. Once you look it in the eye, you have power over it. Once you confront it and see it for what it is, you can take charge of it. He says fear shows in our eyes.

"Don't ever let your fear show," is what Bugsy told me. "You'll always have the edge if they don't see your fear. Just look the dog in the eye. Just look your fear in the eye." I'll never forget that, no matter where I go. I just look it in the eye.

The second thing happened when I was ten. Uncle G, who is also my godfather, surprised me with a pair of ice skates on

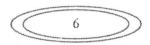

my birthday. Uncle G knew how much I liked Sonje Henie, the best ice skater in the world. She was my idol. I wanted to look like her, wear her costumes, skate like her – I wanted to *be* Sonje. Sonje Henie won more Olympic and World Titles than any other lady figure skater in the world. She was beautiful. I loved my Sonje Henie paper dolls. Mama and I designed beautiful paper costumes. Now I had real ice skates, and Mama and I design real costumes for me. I can be just like Sonje.

Two of Uncle Giovanni's bodyguards – I call them The Bodies – are assigned to take me to ice skating lessons. I was really nervous and scared that I'd fail at being Sonja. But Bugsy reminded me that I'd tamed the Dobermans so I could certainly tame the ice. He didn't realize that part of my fear had nothing to do with the ice. It was fear of life outside the family compound, where I'd not often gone, and had never gone alone.

"Just look it in the eye," Bugsy said and winked at me.

The third thing that changed my life was Sandy. I met Sandy at our first ice skating lesson. Sandy became my best friend. Well, actually, she was my first and only friend. We had our beginner lessons together twice a week, and private ice time three times a week. There were six girls in our class. Sandy and I came the earliest, stayed the latest, and we worked the hardest. We were both crazy about figure skating. I went to the rink every day to practice and meet Sandy. Now, we're competing together. I can't wait to see her today. She'll be as excited as me.

The first time I learned to lace up my skates, Sandy was on the trainer's bench beside me. I looked my fears in the eye, and everything about my life in Wyandotte, Michigan, changed. I was no longer just the niece of Don Salvatore Giovanni, the invisible girl in the big Giovanni Family Compound, playing in an empty playhouse. Now, I lived in a separate world with my friend Sandy and others like us who lived fearlessly on a slab of ice. I've learned that the Dobermans and cracks are just like all of life: loud, fast, and dangerous. I just look them all in the eye. I'm not afraid of the Dobermans, or the cracks in the ice. I'm ready.

Chapter Two

"Gina! Gina!" Mama is calling me. "You are packed, yes? The car is ready. You go now, Gina. Be good girl. Skate good, get prizes."

I run down the curved stairs with my suitcase and skate case dragging behind me bumping down the carpeted stairs.

"Not on the marble, Gina," Mama screams at me to pick them up as I cross the marble foyer. My pink and silver metal skate case bangs against my leg where it's made a permanent bruise on my calf. Mama kisses me on both cheeks, like she always does. I can see The Bodies waiting for me on the porch. They look all shimmery through the thick cut-glass doors. With one Body in front of me and one behind me we move down the steps and into the black car waiting in the portico.

"You're a vision of loverness today, Gina." I don't know where Nick ever heard that, but it's nice of him to say it.

"Here, Gina. Don't say I never did nothin' for ya'." Weasel hands me a good luck Hershey Bar for the car ride.

"Thanks, Weasel."

We drive slowly around the curved driveway of the family compound passing the play yard and stopping at the guard gate. Nick and Weasel stop to talk to Bugsy so I hop out of the car.

"Hi Capu, hi Veloce." The dogs drop in response to my

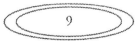

hand signal, and wait to be petted.

"Good luck, Gina," Bugsy calls. "Knock 'em dead, girl, arrivederci."

"Bye, Bugsy!"

"Just look 'em in the eye," Bugsy says and winks at me.

"Bye, Mama," I yell to her and wave as she stands on the portico watching us, and crossing herself. Mama always prays for everybody to be safe and come back alive.

"Bye you guys," I say to the Dobermans. "Wish me luck!" The Bodies slam the car doors shut. I'm so excited I'm wiggling already. Weasel turns and looks at me over his dark glasses. The look says, "Sit still." It's his job.

"Nick and Weasel, today I want you to meet Sandy." Nick pulls onto the highway and I open my Hershey Bar. "Sandy's my best friend. She'll probably be a famous skater someday."

"Yeah, we know which one she is. We don't hafta' meetcher friend. Not parta our job."

"Yeah, we don' socialize none when we's workin'. Boss don' like it." Their boss is my Uncle Giovanni. Everybody wants to please the Boss. Nick has told me to sit still twice already, but I just can't.

"Only a few more miles, Gina. You ready?"

"Yep."

"Scared?"

"Nope."

I've competed in many shows at our rink and around Detroit, in the last three years. Once I went with Sandy to Flint for the Regional Competition. I've won lots of ribbons, trophies, and awards. I've already decided I want to be a professional ice skater after I win the Olympics. My coach thinks I'm going to be good enough. He says I have work ethic, too, and that's important for a champion, he told me. But today's competition is different from the others. This is a huge show in Detroit. It's the State Competition, which is why I'm so excited. It feels different.

From the waiting area I can see all the people in the stands. It's more people than I've ever seen in one place in all my life; more than in the cathedral in Little Sicily where I go to church. My stomach is tracing a 180 figure. The music is playing on an organ that's so loud it tickles my insides. Not like the organ at church. It's a wonder it doesn't crack the ice. It plays all the time; I think I might get a headache. The ice in this big arena has colored designs on it that mark out the field for ice hockey games. We have to ignore those and concentrate on our own figures. This will be hard. I forget to swallow and choke on my spit.

It's different in another way, too. I'm skating on a more advanced level today. Of course, more is expected at this level, so I probably won't win anything this time. That's okay. My coach says I'm just here for the experience. 'Don't be afraid,' he says to me. I won't be. I've been competing since I was eleven, and I've never yet been afraid. I just look my new competition level right in the eye. I take charge, just like Bugsy says.

The locker room is chaos. Locker rooms are always like this at competitions, but this is worse. It's bigger and louder. Girls screech with excitement and help each other with shoulder straps and hair dos. Bobbie pins fly all over the place. Some of the girls cry over disappointing hair dos and complain about costumes that don't fit right. Others run in and out the toilets and at least one is throwing up. Another, having toe spasms, rubs her feet and cries. Mama had pulled my curly black hair into a tight chignon this morning and Mrs. Scarlo put some sparkly jewelry on it. I think it looks good. I have a lot of hair, like Mama. One of the host officials with a wide ribbon dangling from her nametag comes into the locker room.

"Ladies, we welcome you to the competition today. If you need anything at all find someone wearing a ribbon like this and we'll be happy to help you. I have an announcement! The prizes today include a month at Summer Training Camp in Chicago with world class skaters, coaches, and trainers. May I be the first to wish you all good luck?"

World class skaters, coaches and trainers? I'd love to win a trip to Chicago. Everyone knows that the selections for the National Team usually come out of the summer camps, even though no one officially mentions that. So, of course, we all really want to win a place at camp. The locker room fills up with nervous energy. I can almost see it, like fog over the Detroit River. Sandy and I find an empty locker to share and zip each other into our costumes.

"Gina, Gina, I'm so excited. I have to go to the bathroom. How do I look?"

"You look fine, Sandy. Your costume looks great on you. Do I look okay?" I tug on the legs of my costume and check myself out in the mirror. Sandy fills out her costume nicely. She has more shape and curves than I do. Mama says I'm a late bloomer. I stand in front of the mirror and imagine myself on the ice. I can see my entire routine. I look myself in the eye.

"Girl, move! You're hogging the mirror." I blink at the skater who shoves me.

"Sorry," I say, and move away from the mirror.

"That was rude. Who did your makeup?" Sandy asks me.

"Mrs. Scarlo, Uncle G's secretary."

"It looks so professional. Do you think she could do mine next time? I could come over to your place. Your costume is scrumptious, where did you get it?"

"Stop chewing your fingernails, Sandy. Come with me to the restroom."

I grab Sandy's hand and head to the restroom. Asking someone to come to the restroom is the best way to change the subject. Two things I don't want to talk about. First of all, Sandy always wants to come to my house, and now she wants to come to get her makeup done. I can't invite her to my house.

My house is…different. And second, I don't want to talk about my costume. Mama and I made it. We could've bought it from the Columbia Costume Company Catalogue, just like everyone else. If I'd asked Uncle G, he would've said, "whatever you want, Angel Baby. Let's order you two of the finest!" But Mama and I like designing and sewing together. And really, our costumes are prettier and fit better than anyone else's. I don't want anyone to know it's homemade, though. They would laugh at me, and I don't want them to make fun of Mama, either. They'd say we are poor. We aren't poor.

Chapter Three

Sandy and I head back to the locker room. I sit down on the bench and angle my feet into my skates. These are another pair of new boots because I've grown four sizes since I started skating. I lace them up tight with double knots and tuck the ends into the crisscrossed laces. My toes aren't supposed to move. I try wiggling them to check. I take a deep breath to slow my heart rate, and I stare at the toe picks, taking power over them.

Everyone's nerves are on edge. Girls are biting their nails, picking their acne, and scratching their hives. We all have to do something with our tension. I play with my hands pretending to skate my Sonja Henie paper dolls across my lap in time to the music, like I did when I was little. I look into the eyes of my competition, and I wait.

"You girls iz ready now? C'mon, c'mon, get a moof on right now, den." Helga claps her hands and herds us out of the locker room. Helga makes her usual joke about her being Bossy ze Cow leading her young heifers. She's told that joke at every show in the last three years. It isn't really funny anymore, but we all laugh anyway because Helga thinks that's a really funny line, and we all like Helga. She's just trying to settle our nerves with her big voice and her not-so-funny "yokes." It's her "yob."

The chop-chop of our wooden blade covers follow us out to our waiting area. From here we can see the competition and rest while waiting for our warm-up call.

"You remember now, ja? You do not talk or eat in here, ja? No clapping wiz your hands, neither." Helga doesn't have to remind us, we all know the rules by heart, but it's her job. Many of the girls pace: chop, chop, chop, chop, back and forth. Others stretch and warm their muscles. But I want to watch the performances. I want to see the competition.

Hans, Helga's husband is leading the boys out to their waiting area. They gather on the other side of the room. Except for the pairs teams, boys and girls aren't allowed to sit together. Helga and Hans remind us once again that no one is allowed to talk. That's a pretty good plan, actually, because boys like to tease and mess up the girls' hair dos. It also keeps the girls from saying mean things to each other, which they do. It's probably just because they're nervous, but Mama would say their mamas didn't teach them well, 'no manners,' she would say.

For some reason, I start thinking about the boys. I don't really care very much about the boys so I don't know why I'm thinking about them. I wonder what their locker room looks like. I wonder if they're scared, nervous, shriek about their hair and fuss with their costumes. Sandy says the boys' restrooms don't have sit down toilets. She has a brother and she knows things like that. She says the boy skaters don't wear any underwear. Mama would have a fit if I told her that. It's probably not true anyway. I've discovered that girls say a lot of things that aren't always true, especially about boys. Mama says God always expects us to tell the truth.

Even though we spend a lot of time together and we all love skating, most of the skaters aren't really friends. We applaud, smile, and congratulate each other, but we all want to be the best. That's what it's all about, really, being the best. When Sandy and I were about twelve, our trainers talked to us about that very thing.

"Ice skating takes concentration," they told us. "Social skaters aren't serious skaters." But Sandy and I swore a blood oath. We wrote in red nail polish on the inside of our skate cases:

Sandy and Gina 2 best friends 4ever.

I'm glad Sandy and I are friends forever, no matter what. I've told Mama about Sandy, and she's glad I have a friend. Mama says I should pray for Sandy, my best friend. "God bless her," I say. I wish Sandy could come to my house, but only family and business associates come to the compound. It's a good thing Mama never comes with me to the ice rinks. She wouldn't like to hear all the snarling and insulting that goes on among the skaters. Even their mothers do it! Not that Mama would do that, she never would. But she wouldn't like it.

She'd probably get a migraine headache. She'd probably say I should pray for them, too. I don't really want to.

I'd really like to show Mama how well I can skate, but it's good she doesn't come. Her life is at the family compound and she rarely ever leaves it, only for Mass on Sundays and parties in Little Sicily. If I didn't skate, I'd probably be stuck there, too. Mama's afraid to talk to people who might make fun of the way she talks, and she has headaches a lot. Uncle G says Mama keeps a low profile. I used to think that meant she was small, But now I'm older, I think it means she needs to stay home. I like being at home with Mama, sewing and listening to opera. I always think of Mama when I enter the ring, but the ice arena is where I am finally in charge of me.

Chapter Four

The announcer calls for warm ups and Sandy and I charge onto the ice with all the other early skaters. She skates backwards facing me and we grin at each other. We reach out and squeeze each other's hands for just a second, we shout, "Good luck," and we really mean it. We stroke off, building up speed with our crossovers. We do this at every competition. We think it's our lucky charm thing to do, but we have to cross our pinkies and do it in exactly that order, just the same way for the past four years. Mama says I mustn't be superstitious, so I cross myself, too, just to be sure. I can't wait to hear my name called out in the starting order. I'm not afraid at all. The announcer finally calls my name. He says "Gina Mongowli of Wyandotte, Michigan." He messed it up! It's okay. A name isn't really important, is it?

Gliding to the center of the huge arena I pose, listening for my music cue. It starts out loud and fast. The smile is frozen on my face. It's just me, the music, and the ice.

The cold air energizes me. The fast- gliding freedom on the ice is what I love. Moving faster than a girl could ever run it's as if all the energy on earth is pulling and pushing me across the ice. Is this how it feels to run as fast as Veloce? I jump and I'm flying. I could reach a cloud, poke a hole in it, and let the snow sprinkle down onto the ice. Spinning, spinning, spinning – I've already learned to do two really good spins, clean and fast. I swear stars fall all around me sparkling, and twinkling when I spin. I love the ice. It's so smooth, so clean, so perfect. Stretch, balance, breathe, lay back, spin. This is my favorite; I wish Mama could see me. Twirling like the little dancer in Mama's music box, the costume so pretty, Mama would surely be proud to see me. Spinning is like the highest note in the aria on Mama's opera record. Coach says it's climactic. Before the spin is completed, I hear the crowd stamping and clapping.

As soon as they had walked me to the locker room when we arrived, the Bodies had disappeared from sight. But I know they're out there, watching, and when I come out of the locker room after the show they'll just reappear and we'll do our follow-the-leader-bit back to the car. Wherever I go, Weasel is in front of me – looking like another weasel might jump out at him any minute – then comes me and my skate case bruising my leg, and then Nick right behind me to shut us into the car. Weasel says we need to blend in, not stand out in a crowd. I think we're about as inconspicuous as a family of Detroit River ducks crossing the highway.

"Congratulations," the Bodies say at the same time, once we're closed in the car. I smile, show them my prizes, and thank them.

"Did you see Sandy? She was great!"

"Yeah, we seen her. Seen you, too. Nice job."

"I'm exhausted." I sort of snooze off and on happily all the way home, filled to the brim with satisfaction. My ribbons are on my lap, my trophy beside me. I can't wait to show Mama. Nick tosses me a chunk of Double Bubble. I smile at my reflection in the car window and blow bubbles. I wonder what Uncle G will say when he hears my news.

A few months ago, as one of the top twenty skaters in the state of Michigan, my picture was in the paper. I showed it to Uncle G. I thought he'd say, "Nice picture, Angel Baby." But he wasn't real happy for some reason. He poked the picture with his finger and called into his intercom, "Bett! In here." Bett is Mrs. Scarlo, his secretary. She came right in with her steno pad.

"Get Mark Henson on the phone over at the *Detroit Free Press* and remind him what my rules are about this family." He held up the paper, Mrs. Scarlo nodded, and started out. She paused beside me and whispered in my ear, "Nice picture, sweetie." She winked at me and glided out the door in her bright blue, slinky dress and spike heels.

Deanna Klingel

Chapter Five

<u>*Page one of my new diary that Mama gave me for my*</u>
<u>*14th birthday in 1957*</u>

*Dear Secret Friend Diary, Watching the premier skaters
today was the biggest thrill of my life – well, so far, anyway. I
know I will skate forever. The music, the figures, the costumes,
the showmanship, all inspired me. I want to be that good.
Someday I want to skate in the Olympics and then with Holiday
on Ice. My dream!*

This is what happened today in my first hugely enormous
big time competition:

The announcer called Sandy's name. She pulled off her
blade covers and I squeezed her hand. Our coach patted her
shoulder for luck and I showed her that my fingers were
crossed for her. I really hoped Sandy would win. I crossed all
my fingers and held my breath.

Sandy's program was flawless and her figures near
perfect. She included a new loop jump that she's not been
doing for very long and I knew she was nervous about it, but
she landed it perfectly. When she took her curtsy she was

grinning real big, she knew she'd done well. The audience loved her program. Her performance was solid and her required elements marks were good.

I was so excited for her that I almost forgot I still had to skate! Sandy came to the entrance to watch me when it was finally my turn. The announcer messed up my last name, he said Mongowli, instead of Mangalli. It doesn't matter. How important is a name anyway? I flipped off my blade covers and pushed onto the ice. I finished my warm up, took a starting position, and waited for my music cue.

I don't remember too much after that. I heard my music end and felt a huge smile on my face. Was it really over already? I'd landed every jump, every requirement, and my costume felt wonderful. Could the ice ever be smoother? Absolutely no cracks anywhere. I took my curtsy. The shouting, stamping, and applauding roared around the huge arena like thunder during a storm. Flowers rained down onto the ice. My heart was pounding when I skated off and into Sandy's arms. Our coach was jumping up and down and laughing. We waited in the Kiss and Cry area and I leaped out of my chair and into his arms when the judges showed the ordinals. I've never been so happy.

We settled down to watch the rest of the divisions and the pairs. Watching all of them taught me one thing, dear Diary: how much more I have to learn. After the placement awards were made and Sandy and I had both been called to the podium for our awards, the announcement was made for Summer Training Camp selections.

All the skaters were holding their breath and chewing their fingernails. Sandy and I, holding hands, were called to the podium to receive our summer camp credentials along with the others who were being invited. Skaters at all levels, all ages, and from different states are going to camp together. Sandy and I jumped up and down like when we were little girls. We were so happy.

Mama is calling me for dinner. Best Friends 4 Ever, Gina Mangalli

P.S. I'm the new State Junior Figure Skating Champion, 1957. I can hardly believe it! What will Uncle G say?

Deanna Klingel

Chapter Six

"I hardly can believe my eyes, my own daughter. Look at this everybody, a medal, yes? A trophy cup, yes? My daughter the skater, eh, Giovanni, what you say, huh?" Mama grabs Uncle G and kisses him on each cheek, nearly spilling his drink. He laughs.

Mama holds up my certificate decorated with fancy gold letters. I know she's going to hang it on the wall with the others. She calls this wall "My daughter wall, for blue-ribbons-and-trophies-for-being-proud-of-her wall."

"You musta be famous skater now, Gina, yes? You don't letta that go into your head now, you hear me, daughter? You don'ta getta snooty on us now and so you got to say a thank-you to Uncle Giovanni for getting you all those lessons, yes? He musta hear about this, too. You thank God, too. You be good girl, now, Gina. You gotta remember the peons when you are famous." She laughs and kisses both my cheeks. "You a good girl, eh?"

"Yes, Mama."

Uncle G is most interested in hearing how many skaters were there, how many people paid to come and watch, how much the tickets cost, how much to park a car, how many drinks and cigarettes were sold at the arena, how many people worked at the arena, and if there was good security. He looks at the program and calculates how much money came in from entry fees.

"Congratulations, Gina Baby! That's good. You done real good. Being a business man, you know, I can appreciate all this. Sports are getting to be a big business. *Big* business."

Yes, I do know that. But he already has dry cleaning businesses, laundries, bakeries, grocery stores, liquor stores, the County Racing Commission, a gym for boxers, and a protection agency. Maybe he owns a library too; I know he has a book maker who comes on Fridays named Gyro. Is he thinking now about owning an ice rink? He's very busy, and very important. He has a lot of Business Associates. Mama says he's a very successful business man.

I'm not sure how I feel about Uncle G's interest in the ice skating business. I love Uncle G, but I like having my life separate from the family compound. That's probably selfish. But it feels good to be in charge of something on my own.

Mama and the staff have prepared a special celebration dinner. A huge bouquet of bright colored flowers in a silver vase fills the center of the table, and candlesticks gleam in a long straight line. I like how the chandelier reflects off the shiny table. Mama supervised this menu. I can tell she did, because it's all her favorite stuff: mozzarella caprese in the parlor, where Mama, the Associates, and Uncle G have tall goblets of red wine. Uncle Giovanni insists I have a little since the party is in my honor.

"A little taste of life, Angel Baby," he says toasting me like a grown up. The light sparkles through the crystal goblets and ruby red reflections bounce around like little balloons on the walls. Mama speaks to him in Italian; he just laughs and waves her away. I think she's telling him fourteen is too young to toast and drink wine. The wine warms my face and I know my cheeks are rosy. In the dining room with every chair filled, we eat calamari vinaigrette salad, tortellini in broth, cannelloni, bread, gnocchi al pesto, veal saltimbocca and dessert ices, with lots more wine. When Mama goes all out for special dinner parties, Staff and Business Associates are always invited.

At dinner the huge flower vase keeps me from seeing everyone's faces. So I stare at the silver vase. *Who is this girl in the reflection?* I have Mama's pretty hair, and her smooth olive skin tone. Some people say I look like her, but I think Mama's pretty. I look more like a paper doll, flat and thin, with zits on my chin. I hide behind the flowers, and nervously tell the family about being selected for the summer camp. I hope Uncle G will say I can go. Mama will do whatever Uncle G decides. Mama says it's big of him to let me go to the skating rink. What will he think about camp?

"How you go to sleep at the camp, huh?" Mama wants to know where I'll be sleeping and with whom. "You getta germs from sleeping too close," she warns me. "Who'sa gonna be washing up your clothes, huh? For three months? Naw. You got no three months…hmm…ninety pairs you need, ninety pairs unmentionables for three months. You wear only one time, Gina, that's the way, you gotta to wash before you wear again. Mrs. Scarlo goa shop for ninety pairs. You don't got enough nightgowns for three months. You gotta safety pins, huh, Gina? Three months. Hmm. Too long. How you do that? Who take you to church? They gotta church?"

Mama worries and carries on, while The Associates drink and toast my success. Uncle G needs to know exactly where the camp is, what kind of travel arrangements I'll need, and if Nick and Weasel will be enough Bodies. I think they'll be two too many, and I slink further behind the flowers. He asks his Security Staff to check out the area around the camp.

"First thing, Boss." He shovels in Mama's fancy food like he's starved. Mama scowls at his bad manners.

"Your mama never teaches you nice manners, eh? Looky here at my Gina, she's a lady. You a slop." She slaps his head and everyone laughs.

"Coach Darwin says the packet will arrive in the mail and all the answers to your questions will be there." I'm relieved to have told it and relieved there doesn't seem to be a question of whether or not I can go. It sounds like I'm going to go, as long as I have enough emergency safety pins and ninety pair of underwear to satisfy Mama. Of course, I know it might depend on what the Staff finds out about "the area." Everyone kisses my two cheeks and congratulates me again.

"Night, champ!" someone calls.

"Buona notte," everyone says.

My stomach's feeling a little queasy. It might be the huge meal. Could be the wine. Or, it might be that I'm thinking about three months away from Mama. I've never slept away before, ever. I look my pillow in the eye, and then I punch it. I can do this. I close my eyes and skate off to sleep. *Will three months seem long? Or will it go too fast? Will Sandy and I make other friends? Who will wash my clothes?*

Deanna Klingel

Chapter Seven

Going to Summer Training Camp means a train trip to Chicago, Illinois. The farthest away from the family compound that I've ever gone was the Flint and Detroit competitions for the day. But I do know where Chicago is. Uncle G reads the Chicago newspapers. I know we have family there, and Uncle Giovanni has business connections in Chicago. He brought me a little brass Chicago skyscraper once. It was intended to be a paper weight or a bookend. Mama called it a "what nut" and a "dust collector." Uncle G said he had an office in that skyscraper. I hope I'll see it from the train.

I hardly slept last night. It was the last night in my own bed for the next three months. I made several trips to the bathroom – more nervous than before any competition. I competed two more times since the big Detroit show, earned podium positions at both, and I was never scared. But maybe I am a little scared this morning about going away to camp. I don't even want breakfast. I stare at my trunk. Look it right in the eye. I look into my own eyes in the mirror. No one will know I'm afraid. I open my skate case and look at Sandy's promise. I'll bet Sandy's nervous and scared today, too, about going to camp. But Sandy has gone to church camp and to stay with her Grandma for a week every summer. I've never slept away.

My big blue trunk is filled with everything on the packing list. Mama's added extra of everything. She's sure I can't survive on only that list. I have extra nightgowns, extra underwear, twice as many socks, and two bathing suits in case one doesn't dry fast enough. She sent an extra towel to be sure I don't borrow one. She put in an entire package of safety pins in case my hems come out or straps break. Mama packed three sacks of biscotti in case they don't feed me enough. She found this orange juice powder at Del Ponte's Store and said if they didn't give me fresh fruit every day I should mix this with water so I wouldn't get scurvy.

"Mama, I'm not going to sea."

"You listen to Mama. Mamas know about some things."

"Yes, Mama."

The car pulls up to the portico and I hear voices down below. I skip down the long staircase and pass Nick going up to get my trunk. This black car is just one of several Uncle Giovanni owns.

All the black cars are parked in a row and kept locked up in the garage that is almost as long as the big house. The Garage Boys and the Pit Crew (mechanics) all work there. Some of them went to school over the garage with the tutors when they were younger. Someone is always on guard duty at the garage. They're guarding the cars and the arsenal. I used to think they were guarding the school books, but now I'm older, I know more.

Once I asked him, "Uncle G, wouldn't you just once like to ride in a red car? All your boring black cars look just alike."

"If you ride in a red car, Bambino, everyone will remember seeing you. Riding in black cars keeps them guessing. No one's ever quite sure if they saw you, where you are, where you've been, or where you're going. See that? Huh? When you see a red car you look right in there and notice who's in it, don't you? Sure you do. What kind of hat they wear, who they're with, all that? Right? Red cars are interesting. When you see a black car, who cares? Huh? Got that? See how that works? It's all about privacy, see? Black cars and privacy make for better business practices. Black, Angel Baby, always black." I shrugged and pretended I understood. I'd never ridden in a red car, so what did I know about that anyway?

He made the car business sound simple, but I knew it wasn't. The Garage Boys and Pit Crew all have special jobs and they are always busy. Their jobs are all called Insurance. Several of them, or their kids, the *cuscinos* – cousins – come to the compound school above the garage, where I go to school. Before backing out a car they put on a new license plate that snaps on with magnets. One time one of the cousins brought a pocketful of those magnets upstairs to science class so the tutor could explain how magnets work. I guess with changing the license plates, it's like Uncle G said, no one is ever quite sure who's been seen where. If you're a business man like Uncle G, that's important. Mama says we're so lucky to have a private school education for our family, and so much employment.

This morning, the Garage Boy called Dannu – in Sicilian that means Damage – slaps a new license plate over the old one, the Bodies load my trunk, the Pits check the engine and the undercarriage to be sure it's clean. Mama kisses me on both cheeks and reminds me to be good, say my prayers, and always wear clean underwear. Then the Bodies drive me to the train station.

Other skaters, coaches, and team members from our own arena are already here. I'm surprised to see some of the older skaters from Detroit who didn't win an invitation. They're paying lots money to go to the camp, Sandy says.

"Sandy, look over there by the bench. No, over there. Don't stare. See the man with the cap? His picture is hanging in the arena next to the pictures of Ulrich Salchow, Werner Rittberger, Karl Schafer, and Sonja Henie. He must be a famous skater, too. Who is he?"

"Oh, yeah, I've seen his picture. I don't know who he is but we should get an autograph."

"No, don't, that's embarrassing."

"No, it isn't. It's a compliment." She grabs a pen out of her bag and walks right over, not one bit embarrassed. Sandy is so in charge, even off the ice. I'd like to be like that. This is truly going to be the most exciting summer of my life. I can hardly swallow, and I sure can't keep still. I hop first on one leg, then the other. I sway to music in my head. I wish Sonja Henie could be at camp. That would really be the icing on the cake.

"Alll Abooooaaarrd...

"Gina, come on, let's go." Sandy has two autographs in her hand.

Deanna Klingel

Chapter Eight

Dear Diary, I'm home from camp. I'm looking out the window, watching the Dobermans. I'll tell you all about camp a little later, but right now I don't feel like talking. Gina

It's too painful to write about, but I keep reliving it in spite of myself.

Summer camp turned out to be like a great big, wonderful, chocolate cake that just before you get to eat it gets ruined with something nasty – like coffee icing.

The delicious layers – all the things I learned – things like washing my own clothes, trying new food, and having friends, made the most wonderful summer like a great dessert. We each had assigned times to use the laundry room and no one did it for you. I heard campers complaining about this, but for me it was new and exciting. I've never washed clothes before. I'm not even sure who washes our clothes at the family compound. Maybe it's Mrs. Pristas the housekeeper, or maybe Mama. It just gets done.

I learned about different places that I've not heard about before. We even had two Russian skaters with us for our first month. Martinka and Pascha were the most beautiful dancers

I'd ever seen. They practiced their routines on the wooden
dance floor before going onto the ice. They slid across the ice
light as feathers. My coach says ballet lessons help with skating
and so we had ballet class every day with Martinka and Pascha.
I'm going to ask Uncle G if I can take dancing lessons. He'll
probably say, "Anything for you, Angel Baby."

Each night for dinner the meal celebrated a different state,
the home of one of the campers. One night after dinner I wrote
Mama a letter about eating lobsters from Massachusetts where
Margaret and John live. I think they're kind of boyfriend and
girlfriend. They don't skate pairs, but they hang on each other
like they do. I didn't tell Mama that part. I'm not sure she'd
understand that they're in high school. I wonder if I'll have a
boyfriend in high school? How can I if my school is over the
garage? Most of the boys I know are stupid or greasy anyway.
I've asked Mama if I can go to public high school with Sandy.
She's thinking about it. She smiled. I think that's a yes.

The best part of the dining room at camp was Freda Rose.
All the cafeteria ladies were grumpy except Freda Rose. Freda
Rose knots her hair net on her forehead; it looks like a fly
sitting there. Some of the girls made fun of her, but I didn't.
Mama wouldn't want me to do that. She says if you're unkind
it doesn't matter if you're pretty, you will still be ugly. If
you're kind you always look pretty, Mama says.

The first time I went through the line, Freda Rose smiled
at me and said, "Now ain't you just the prettiest little skater

girl. I bet you're a picture out there with all that hair. How 'bout that." She laughed and gave me an extra spoon of mashed potatoes. So, after that I always spoke to her nicely at every meal. She'd laugh and throw on a little extra. She thinks I'm going to be a star. She says it's written in my stars and she can read the stars.

I had private coaching every day and private ice time for practice. We learned about levels of proficiency, scoring, judging, and all the competitions required for advancing to the Championships. We had choreography class, music class, and I learned to dance. I've learned so many things that I didn't even know I needed to know. It was great and Sandy and I had more fun than we've ever had.

I couldn't wait to tell Mama and Uncle G about how I learned to "interpret the music." They both like to listen to opera on Uncle G's records. Now I can interpret it with dance movements. I learned to hear the music, feel the music, and then become the music – on ice. I planned to show them in the parlor. I've seen Uncle G dance at parties and weddings and when he whirls around with a lady the other dancers stop to watch them. He's a good dancer and he likes music. Maybe Uncle G will dance with me. Well, that's what I thought might happen. But it didn't happen that way. Not at all.

"Sandy, can you believe these three months have gone by already? I heard girls talking about the big end-of-camp show. I can't wait!"

"I know. My group is working on something really neat. It is going to be *THE* best!"

"The closing reception is really a big deal," one of the campers interrupted. "I heard they always have a surprise. Off to the laundry, excuse me." She pushed past us.

"Gina, did you see the sports page of the newspaper? All the interviews we did the other day are in there. Did you cut it out? Did you know they were scouting us? My mom and dad won't believe this. I feel like we're famous or something."

"I cut it out, too. I want to show it to Mama. She won't believe that important skating people from all over the country came just to watch us. I cut out the one that said I was an "up and comer to be watched." Mama will like that. They spelled my name wrong – Gena."

Everyone performed with their group at the closing show. It was so great! At the big reception we had punch and cupcakes that had little skates made of icing plopped on the tops. Sandy and I both saved our icing skates and wrapped them in paper napkins to take home. I wanted to keep mine forever, and I wanted to show it to Mama.

Then the master of ceremonies tapped on his punch glass.

"May I have your attention please, campers?" *Ssshhh.* "We have a special surprise guest speaker this afternoon. A great finale to a wonderful camp. Will you give a warm welcome to … *ta dah* … Miss Sonja Henie."

I was so surprised I gasped and inhaled a piece of my cupcake. It stuck in my throat and I coughed so much that Sandy beat me on the back and then someone else made me drink some punch and I coughed more and the punch came out my nose, all over the table, and someone else pulled my arms up and I gagged and thought I might throw up. It was only a little crumb of cake, but I couldn't get it up. I coughed and coughed and everyone was looking at me, pounding my back, pulling my arms above my head, and asking if I was okay, and then my trainer came over and took me out of the room. I was slobbering, and it was all so embarrassing, I thought I would just die.

By the time I stopped coughing and clearing my scratchy throat, my eyes were all red, my nose was running, and Sonja Henie was finished talking. Everyone was applauding and standing up when I got back to the room; she was stepping down off the dais. She left the room with two men. She was so beautiful, so elegant, and it was over. I had missed it. My idol was right in the very room where I was sitting – and I missed it. I felt all empty and dry, wrinkly and ugly – like a raisin. I plopped down in my chair, threw my napkin on the floor, and pouted. I couldn't stop the tears. The cake tasted awful in my mouth. I just don't want to talk about it.

Deanna Klingel

Chapter Nine

Instead of being all chatty and happy when we walked back to our dormitory room, I was sullen and miserable. Sandy giggled and talked about it all the way back. I wanted to tell her to shut up, but she had a right to be happy. *She* had seen Sonja Henie in person.

"You know, Gina, Sonja Henie isn't as young as she used to be. She's not the best anymore, you know. Other skaters are doing newer stuff." Sandy tried to make me feel better, but she just shattered the heart that loved Sonje.

Before we got to our dormitory, two local boys who'd been walking behind us started acting really noisy and obnoxious. One of them made a siren noise and ran in circles around us, like he was a police car. The second one pretended to be shooting a Tommy gun at us. He hopped around us in a circle aiming his pretend gun, complete with staccato sound effects.

"Knock it off," Sandy shouted. "Why are you being so stupid? Get out of our way."

I was still so mad about missing Sonja Henie that I hardly noticed them and kept right on walking.

"We just wanted to see what the *niece* of the infamous Don Giovanni – *of Little Sicily* – would do if she heard the cops coming. Packing any heat, *Princess*?" He was talking very sarcastic and I didn't like it one bit. But he got my attention.

Sandy put her hands on her hips. I stood still with my mouth gaping.

"What the heck are you talking about? Get out of our way. Why should we care about your stupid cop siren? Come on Gina, we're going." She grabbed my arm and we ran the rest of the way. The boys didn't give chase, but they laughed so loud we still heard them when we ran up the steps of our dormitory. *They think they're really funny. But – what did they say about my uncle? How do they know about Uncle G? Little Sicily? How do they know who I am?*

We were out of breath after running up to our third floor room. We flopped down on our beds, gasping. Then we laughed, just a little bit, because we always laugh together when we're out of breath.

"Gina, what do you think they were laughing about? How do they know your uncle, anyway?"

"I don't know. We go to Little Sicily for church and parties. But Uncle G doesn't live there."

"What did they mean about the cops and cop cars and all that?"

I shrugged. "I don't know. We only have black cars."

"Well, if I see those wiseacres tomorrow I'm going to demand an explanation. That was just not nice at all. I can't believe how rude some stupid, immature boys can be.

Sometimes I wonder why God made boys anyway."

"Sandy, I don't care. I don't know who those boys are and we'll never see them again. We go home in a few days. Forget it, okay? I'm really tired. Camp's been great, but I'm ready to go home. I'll never get over how I *almost* got to hear Sonje Henie talk." I snagged the tear before it dropped to my cheek.

We didn't see the boys again until we were waiting for our train in Chicago two days later. Sandy and I were sharing a black cow – a root beer with vanilla ice cream in it – when they showed up. One of them placed his hands flat on our table next to our soda and bent over close to us.

"Having a little *mafia* meeting, *Princess*, or can any law abiding citizen join you?" He made a smug little smile and I wanted to slap him. That's the second time he'd call me a princess and he didn't say it like a compliment.

"I told you guys to leave us alone," Sandy shouted loudly. The man in the next booth looked over.

"Anything wrong, young lady?" the man asked.

I started to say no, that nothing was wrong. I was pretty embarrassed. But Sandy stood right up and said, "Yes, sir. Could you kindly ask these boys to leave our table? They weren't invited and they're being a nuisance."

The man stood up. He was at least six feet tall and very filled out. He was handsome and big enough to worry the boys. He opened his jacket and flashed a badge at them.

"It sounds to me like the young ladies have made

themselves clear, fellas. You'd best be on your way."

The boy took his hands off our table and stepped aside. His friend backed away.

"We weren't doin' anything wrong. We just wanted to talk to the niece of *Don Salvatore Giovanni.*"

He said Uncle G's name real loud and very plain. Now other people were looking at us and I wanted to crawl under the table. I whispered to Sandy, "Let it go."

The man put his badge back inside his jacket and looked at me, like he was memorizing my face. Then he said to the boys, "I don't think you have any business here. These young ladies are enjoying their ice cream soda. I don't want you bothering them again. Capice?"

"Yes, sir." They took off. One of them looked back over his shoulder and made some kind of gesture to me. Sandy saw it, gasped, and put her hand over her mouth. She looked shocked.

"Ladies." The man gave us a little salute with his fingers. He sat back down in his booth as if nothing had happened.

"Thank you, sir," Sandy called to him.

My tongue wrapped around my tonsils and I couldn't talk. I just stared at Sandy. A million thoughts were skating through my head, spinning in and out of my brain, faster and faster, keeping up with the rhythm of my heart's pounding. *They've called me a princess twice. They know Uncle G's name. All of it: Don Salvatore Giovanni. So what? He's a business man.*

Maybe he's famous. What was the siren for? Why did he pretend to shoot me? The detective stared at me. He knew Uncle G's name too, I could tell. What about Little Sicily? Is that something besides a place to go to church or have a party? I want to go home. Hurry up train. I want to see Uncle G. No, I don't. I want to ask him about this. I don't like secrets. No, I don't want to know. I've missed Mama. I've missed Capu and Veloce. No, I haven't. Why do we need them to keep people away? Why can't friends come to visit? Why do we have to be so private? How many family secrets do the Dobermans guard? What are those secrets? How do those boys know anything about my uncle? And what exactly do they know about him? The thoughts took on a dance beat. I could skate to that tempo: who, why, what, where, who, why, what, where. Who am I? Why am I protected? What *is* the family compound? And now I'm spinning a perfect spin: GiovanniGiovanniGiovannisecretsecretsecret. My life was unraveling. I heard Sandy slurping up the last bit of soda from the bottom of our glass. It sounded like a blade edge scraping to a sudden stop on the ice. When our train was called, Sandy shook my arm, knocking my elbow off the table.

"Let's go, Gina. That's us. We'll be home in a few more hours."

"Yeah. Right. Okay." I picked up my skate case and my bag. The box of Boston Baked Beans that I bought in a vending machine rattled in the bag. Boston Baked Beans are Bugsy's favorite candy and I had bought them just for him. The bag also held my ticket, my baggage claim, comb, a tiny pillow, aspirin, and a skating magazine to read on the train.

"Yeah, I'm ready." The whole wonderful three months was dissolving inside me while the skate case bruised my leg. We found our compartment and shortly after we got settled two of the Grosse Point skaters sat down and joined us. They were in high school so I was surprised they wanted to sit with us. We talked about the camp and all the great things we'd seen and learned. We talked about skate blades and toe picks, the best boot manufacturer, costume companies, and skaters we admired. One of the girls said she's madly in love with David Jenkins, a great skater. We all like Carol Heiss. We sounded like professionals, like we really knew what we were talking about. I didn't mention Sonja Henie. Sandy had said she was old news. I felt like I'd betrayed a friend.

I was still struggling with missing Sonja Henie, a scratchy throat, the insulting boys, the mysterious man, and Sandy. Even Sandy was starting to get on my nerves. She's always so happy, and so sure of herself. Well, she got to see Sonja Henie, she should be happy. I pulled out my little pillow, put it against my neck, and dropped my head against the window. Rudely, I pretended to be asleep.

I heard them discussing the boys. The older girls talked about how the costumes look on the boys and which ones have the nicest complexions, the most pimples, which ones smoke, who they'd like to go to the movies with, who they'd like to skate pairs with.

"I could look good with Sergio's arms around me," one of them said and they all laughed. "Whooeee!"

Sandy and I hadn't ever talked much about any of this boy stuff before, and I really didn't care to. But she wanted to be a part of the conversation. I suppose it made her feel older. So she talked about the boys who'd insulted me and she told the girls what the boys said – all of it. I wanted to strangle her. But I pretended to be asleep so I didn't have to say anything.

"I can't imagine why they said all that," Sandy said quietly. "And poor Gina, she was mortified."

They all lowered their voices because I was sleeping. They were almost whispering. With one ear pressed against the window and the other hearing the rumble of the train and conversations from other compartments, I had trouble hearing their whispers. They moved closer together with their backs towards me.

"The boys were just awful, and poor Gina had no idea what they were talking about. And thank goodness that detective just happened to be there and stepped up to the situation."

"Is Salvatore Giovanni really Gina Mangalli's uncle?" whispered Rachel.

"Of course," Sandy replied. "So what? Who cares?"

"Does she really not know who he is?" I peeked out one

eye. Sarah's brown eyes were wide and she looked incredulous. "How could she not know?" she almost blurted aloud.

"Shh," Sandy cautioned. "Who is he, then?"

"What? You don't know?"

"If I knew, would I be asking? Come on, tell me. What's the big deal anyway?"

"Don Salvatore Giovanni is in the newspaper every day. Don't you get the *Detroit Free Press* in Wyandotte? He's the Mafia Don, for cryin' out loud. He runs the big crime underground centered in Little Sicily, right there in Wyandotte. A crime family! Didn't you know that? Don't you read the paper? He's the *mafia*!"

"How do you know this?"

"We have Civics in high school. We study current events, and we read the *Free Press* in class. We talk about these things all the time. Giovanni has been subpoenaed to testify at some hearings in Washington D.C. He's boss of some big organized crime syndicate that's being investigated. He's famous. Or is it infamous? I can't believe you don't know about him."

Mafia? Crime family? Syndicate? Underground? Supboena? Uncle G? Crime Boss?

Then I heard Sandy whisper. "Well, we just read *Junior Scholastic Newspaper* in our Junior High. I didn't know that it was her uncle who was the boss. But I know Gina doesn't know anything about all that. Gina doesn't go out to regular school. Except for ice skating and going to church with her family, she never leaves their family's compound. She has her school right there. She says it's a private school. I know she doesn't have the faintest clue about this. And you can't tell her." I wanted to jump up and hug Sandy. She really is my best friend forever.

"Well, someone should tell her and wise her up," whispered one of the girls, but I can't make out which one it is. "For her own good, she needs to know. She could be in danger. I'll bet that FBI detective didn't just *happen* to be there."

FBI? Detective? What detective?

"No!" Sandy blurted, then covered her mouth and went back to her whisper. "No! You cannot tell her. It'll destroy her. She loves her uncle and except for her mother, he's all the family she has. Don't tell her, please. She's safe enough inside the family compound."

"You two must be Queens of Naïveté if you believe that." She spoke in a normal speaking voice and their conversation was over. I sat up, stretched my neck, and pretended to just be waking up.

"My neck is stiff. What did I miss?"

"Nothing, just idle girl chatter, you know."

"Oh, more boy talk?"

"Yes, that's right," Sandy answered too quickly. "More boy talk. You didn't miss a thing. I think I'll take a little nap myself. Could I use your neck pillow, Gina?"

My insides felt like they had pus in them. Like a big

infection spreading fast inside my body; like a crack in the ice that starts out small and spreads, creating dangerous weak places. I swallowed some aspirin, handed Sandy my pillow, and turned my attention to the window. I chewed my lip and tasted the blood in my mouth. The high school girls from Grosse Point were quiet. I wanted to disappear.

Chapter Ten

When our train pulled into the station in Detroit, Nick was there waiting, but I didn't see Weasel. Instead, a new guy stepped out of the shadows and led the way to the car. I waved good bye to Sandy, but she didn't see me because she was being hugged by her mother, father, her little sister, and two brothers. I watched them for just a minute But for some reason, it made me feel sad. *It would be nice to have someone hug me.* So, I stepped between Nick and the new Body and marched straight to the black car without looking at all the hugging families. I walked fast with my head down – in case someone might recognize me as the niece of Don Salvatore Giovanni my trusted godfather and uncle. *But who is he, really?* Nick reached into his pocket and tipped the Red Cap some change for my trunk. I saw the bulge under his coat. It's part of his uniform. I wanted to share my camp experience, share that big delicious cake. I tried to make friendly conversation in the car, but it seemed I was the only one looking for any conversation.

Finally Nick said, "Gina, Princess, this here's Vinny. He's your new Body."

"Nick, don't you ever call me Princess again," I screamed. "I mean it."

"Sure. Sorry." The icing on my great camp cake was

sliding off. It was tasting ickier and looking uglier.

When we got to the family compound I was excited to see Mama. I wanted to feel excited about seeing Uncle G, but I wondered if I'd ever be able to look into his great blue eyes again and see only my handsome uncle. *Who else would I see?*

Veloce and Capu bounded to the gate. They recognized the black car and greeted us. I wanted to get out and see them, but everyone seemed so somber I decided to sit tight. The Dobermans' ears were up, but they stood motionless. Inside the guard house, Weasel waved us through.

"Why is Weasel in the guard house? Where's Bugsy?"

"Bugsy ain't here no more."

"Why? Where is he?"

"Ain't nobody's business."

The huge iron black gate with the fancy gold G opened automatically to welcome us back. I hopped out of the car, and pushed open the heavy front door expecting Mama to be in the foyer. I wanted her to kiss both my cheeks and ask me all about camp. But she wasn't there. No S's – Securities – were at the front door, or in the hall. No one was in the hall at all. The big house was quiet. I dashed off to the staff room and knocked on the door. No one. I ran towards the kitchen. Mrs. Scarlo hurried down the hall toward me.

"Oh, Child, you're home!" She must have forgotten I'm going into real high school in a few weeks. I'm not a child anymore. I'm fifteen.

"Mrs. Pristas, bring some milk and cookies, please. Come in, Gina, let's have a seat. I want to hear all about your summer. I'm so happy you're home."

If they're so happy to see me then why isn't any one smiling? What's that awful noise?

"Where's Mama? Where's Bugsy? Where's Uncle G?" I guess I really did want to see him too, and I wanted to give the box of Boston Baked Beans to Bugsy. I hoped someone might want to hug me and kiss both my cheeks.

"Oh, they're around, Gina. Let's just sit a moment and talk a bit first." I felt her gray dismal mood draping over me like a sweaty, poor fitting costume. Her fake smile didn't fool me. I knew I didn't want to hear this. I wrapped my ankles around the chair legs so tight they hurt. The tension in my body pulled everything inside tight.

"Gina ... darling, something has happened while you were away. It's your Mama, dear. She's ... she's gotten very ill. Giovanni is with her, and her nurse. They're all in the back parlor. She—"

I tore off to the back parlor. I wished I could skate down this long hallway of Oriental carpeting.

"Gina, no wait, I need to tell you something before you—"

I threw open the French doors.

"Mama!"

Deanna Klingel

Chapter Eleven

I had heard of polio. Every summer Mama and I lay down and took a rest in the afternoons so we wouldn't get polio. I guess she didn't do that since I was at camp. *I should have been here.* Former President Roosevelt rode in a wheelchair because he'd had polio. Would Mama need a wheelchair? *I should have been here.*

Mrs. Pristas came huffing into the room. She was out of breath and looked as pale as the white milk and flat sugar cookies. She sat the plate on the library table. No one seemed interested.

Mrs. Scarlo touched me all over as if she saw a dozen bleeding wounds where she needed to apply pressure. She apologized to Uncle G for my being there. She fiddled with my arms, looking at me. I wanted to shake her hands off me, except I couldn't move. I stared at Sister Gertrude who sid the rosary. Sister runs "The Home" where we sent my outgrown clothes. "For the children of less fortunates, God bless them," Mama always said. Mama's crystal rosary beads lay still in her hand. The beads look like ice chips that will never melt.

"It's going to be all right, Gina. Are you … are you okay? Would you like a chair?"

Was someone talking to me? Or was that *thing* talking to

me. It breathed in and breathed out like some huge yellow metal monster. Breathe in ... snap ... breathe out ... whoosh ... breathe in .... But the monster's face was my mother's. The nurse touched me. *Why does everyone want to touch me?* In my head I heard me shout, "Stop touching me!" But no one else heard it.

"My name is Mrs. Baker. You must be Gina. I'm your mother's nurse. Would you like me to explain all of this to you?"

I must have nodded my head yes, but I don't remember doing that. She walked me out, down the hall to a small room off the butler's pantry where we sat down. My hands were cold and my knees trembled. My vision blurred through the gathering tears. She told me about Mama's iron lung keeping her alive, breathing for her. She said it might not be forever. Mama's very brave and not afraid, she said. She might get well. I hope she said that. She held my hands and said a prayer.

I'd barely unpacked my trunk and put all my things away that week before a hearse came to take Mama away. The iron lung was quiet and in a few days it was taken away, too. It weighed almost 500 pounds and was 7 feet long. The room was suddenly very empty, with dents in the floor to remind us what had been there. I spent the day sitting on the floor absorbing the nothingness. I was as empty as the room. I had dents, too, where Mama used to be. I lay on my bed and stared at the

ceiling, where I saw nothing. I looked out the rear window of
the breakfast room, and there was Mama's clothesline. It was
empty too.

It was storming when Nick held the umbrella for me and
Uncle G to go into the Cathedral of All Saints in Little Sicily.
Uncle G wore his black suit, black shirt, black tie, black shoes,
black fedora, and black glasses. He didn't need those glasses
today, but they're part of the outfit. He was surrounded by all
the Bodies wearing all the same black stuff. They surrounded
me, too. I wore a black dress, black cardigan, black dress
pumps, black tights, black gloves, and black lace mantilla on
my head. Mrs. Scarlo had laid the clothes out for me, but I
don't remember putting them on. She brushed my long, black,
hair; I wore it down, curled. Mama would like that.

Uncle G's arm was wrapped around my shoulders so snug
that we moved on the same foot like we were shadow skating
together. I couldn't tell if he was using me to hold himself up
or if he was holding me up. That's how a good skate pair is –
you can't tell.

I love the inside of the Cathedral. I've gone there every
Sunday of my life; lots of Masses, lots of baptisms, and
weddings. It's so bright and golden it always looks like the sun
is shining inside, reflecting its light on everything.

When we entered the church, Uncle G took off his fedora
and handed it to Nick. Uncle G's slick black hair, parted down
the center, stood up on the crown, mussed up by the hat. We

must have looked like a black storm cloud passing through the golden light of the church as we moved down the center aisle. This dark cloud of people moved through the light of the church that was now full of black everything. It was like looking down a hole in the ice in the Detroit River into something bottomless, black and cold.

I heard some of what the priest said about Mama. I saw lots of people wiping their eyes and noses. Uncle G took out his handkerchief and blew his nose a few times. I had always sat next to Mama in our pew; now she was up in front with the black cloth draped over her coffin, surrounded by roses and incense. The priest asked God to receive Carmen Vittoria Maria Giovanni Mangalli into heaven. I said, "Amen."

At the cemetery, a hundred people stood around under their umbrellas all trying to fit under the tent. Everyone wanted to touch me and hug me and bless me. They acted like I'd done something good. I guess they hadn't figured out yet that it was my fault Mama got polio and died. I should have been there. Nick and What's His Name, my new Body, hovered around me and four other Bodies like the gargoyles on the garage roof surrounded Uncle G. I couldn't think of any reason why the Business Associates, Pits, Garage Boys, Bodies, and Gargoyles would need to bring guns to the cemetery in the rain. But there they all were, pretending they hadn't, and pretending that no one noticed the bulges. When they talked about packing, they didn't mean a suitcase for camp. It was another family secret –

just a big fat family secret hidden under their black, dripping trench coats.

And that's how my wonderful layer cake – my summer at camp – slid into the rain at the cemetery. Camp just didn't turn out how I wanted it to.

It's still hard to talk about, dear diary.

Deanna Klingel

Chapter Twelve

It's been a few weeks since Mama's funeral. Sometimes it
seems like a long time ago. Other times it seems like yesterday.
Mrs. Scarlo is ordering a car this afternoon and she and I are
going to drive into Detroit to shop at Hudson's Department
Store for my school clothes. How can we think about school
clothes, I wonder? Is everyone else forgetting my mama? This
is the first time I've ever gone shopping for my own clothes,
and I wanted to be excited. My new clothes always came
delivered from the dressmaker. Mama and Mrs. Scarlo usually
made the designs and Mama often sewed them. My thoughts
are full of pretty colors and soft textures, and clothes I will try
on and choose for myself. I want Mama to be here now
planning my clothes, picking them out together. I'm so anxious
this morning I can hardly eat breakfast. Mrs. Scarlo says we'll
have lunch on the top floor restaurant of Hudson's, another first
for me. And, in another week, it'll also be my first time at
public school. I'm looking forward to riding on the bus with
Sandy to the high school. Mama said I could go to regular
school this year, even though Uncle Giovanni thinks it's not a
good idea. He said we'd respect Mama's wish. I'm going to
have pretty sweaters and blouses, a raincoat, and some
fashionable slacks.

The Hudson Department Store elevator lady wearing white gloves pulls the elevator gate and doors closed. We're headed to the girls' floor for school clothes. There are so many mannequins, so many pretty clothes, I hardly know where to begin.

"May I help you, young lady?" The clerk is speaking to me. Mrs. Scarlo hands the clerk a paper.

"Oh, well, I see you are going to the Cranbook School. Well, right this way to the uniform department and we'll get you all set up."

"Cranbrook School? What uniform?" I scowl at Mrs. Scarlo. "There must be a mistake. Mama said I could go to school with Sandy."

"It'll be best this way, you'll see," Mrs. Scarlo said. "You'll thank me someday."

"But Mama said—

"Mama's not here, dear."

The tears ran over and down my cheeks.

The list included gray pleated skirts, plain white blouses with an emblem, a neck tie, cardigans, and knee socks in two colors, brown saddle oxford shoes, brown leather bag, navy gym bloomers, bathing suit, bathing cap; winter coat, hat, and muffler all with the school emblem, underwear, slips, and other unmentionables, nightgown, robe, slippers, and a chapel cap. I also need the official school blazer, white gloves, stockings with garter belt, a key ring, and a wrist watch with a brown leather band. I look longingly through my tears at the stacks of colorful blouses and sweater sets that would not be mine, and clothes I'd not be choosing for myself.

"Will I be sleeping there?" I ask when I see the nightgown, robe, and slippers.

"Of course, Dear. Cranbrook is a boarding school. You're a very lucky girl. You'll get a wonderful education, and you'll be well prepared for college and marriage."

"College and ma—" I can't even say the word.

"I'm not going to college," I argue, "and I'm not getting married. I'm going to skate." I stamp my foot for emphasis, but Mrs. Scarlo doesn't notice. "I'm going to the Olympics and then I'll join Holiday on Ice and travel around the world. And I'm going to public high school. Mama said I could." My voice is loud and not lady-like; I feel the heat rising in my neck and face. The clerk is pretending she doesn't see this.

Mrs. Scarlo stands tall with her arms crossed gracefully across her chest. She looks surprised that I sassed her. I never did that.

"Where would you have gotten a foolish idea like that?" she asks.

My face is hot and my stomach is in a knot; I bite my lip angrily. The clerk was wrapping everything in tissue paper and stacking them in boxes with the store design. The blazer is in a bag and hangs from a hanger. She ties the boxes together with a little handle, one stack for Mrs. Scarlo, one stack for me. Mrs.

Scarlo thanks her and picks her stack up by the handle. She motions to me to pick up the other. I don't want it. I don't want any of it. I pick it up and let it droop clumsily in my hand.

I like to read and my tutor says I'm bright, but I really hadn't thought much about education. It's just something to do when I'm not skating. Sandy talks about school, and I want to go with her. But Sandy won't be at this boarding school; I won't be riding the school bus. Mrs Scarlo chatters about my wonderful educational opportunities. *Who cares?*

At the rink, I tell Sandy my news. She's as disappointed as me. She says she wanted us to have matching slacks to wear to the football games at the high school. She acts like she's mad at me, like it's my fault. I don't even have any slacks. But if I could go to school with her, I could get some.

"I'm sorry," I say to her. "I really wanted to. But I can't."

"Well, there's nothing we can do about it," she says all huffy. "Everyone knows the mob runs this town and if Giovanni says you'll go, then by golly, you'll go."

"What do you mean by that, Sandy? You know I want to go to public high school with you. I want to ride the bus with you. I want to wear slacks and go to the football games. This isn't my idea. It isn't my fault." I don't want to cry, but the tears are too fast for me.

"Just keep pretending you don't know, Gina. I would too, if I were you." She turns her back on me and just walks away. My only friend just walks away. I feel a big, cold crack spreading across my frozen heart.

When Nick and Vinny come for me, I run out, fling open my own car door, and slam it shut before they even have time to get out of the car. I slide down low in the seat so no one can see me.

"Don't talk to me," I growl at Nick when he looks over the seat at me. He shrugs and looks away.

I should be excited about going off to school. If Mama were here she would have made it exciting. But then, if Mama were here I wouldn't have to go. I miss her terribly. My life seems very confusing right now. Sandy's making it easier for me to leave her, my best and only friend. She ignores me every day at the rink and talks to everyone else. She wears this fake smile pretending she's having such a good time with everyone else. But I know her real smile. Every time I open my skate case I see our little promise written in nail polish. I know she sees it in her skate case, too. Now, all the parts of my heart are melting.

Uncle G often has dinner with me and asks me questions about the skating rink. I answer his questions as politely as I can, but every day I feel angrier with him. Is he really who people say he is? Is he really in the business of crime? Is it his fault Sandy doesn't want to be my friend? Is it his fault I haven't any other friends? Does he miss Mama? Does he know how much I miss her?

Uncle G is the kindest man in the world, Mama always

said. He gives lots of money to charities and churches, and he sends flowers to people in the hospitals, even if he doesn't know them. Mama said he takes care of widows. He buys raffle tickets from the Police Benevolent Society, the Knights of Columbus, and the firemen. He calls me Angel Baby. He takes good care of all his family at the compound, and he takes care of lots of other people, too. I have even heard him say to Bugsy, "Take care of him," and Bugsy says, "Sure, Boss."

So which part isn't true? Who is he really? A little shiver wiggles up my spine right up to the cowlick on my hairline. Who is my handsome uncle? What is he really? Maybe I don't want to know. I'm ready to leave. I think he'll miss me when I'm away at school. Who'll eat dinner with him now that Mama's gone? There are twenty chairs around the table. The two of us sit alone at one end of the long table in the dining room. It's the king-sized version of my lonely play house.

I'll miss the Business Associates who always have time to speak to me. They congratulate me after competitions, and send me flowers. I'll miss the Staff that arranges everything for me, and drinks toasts to me, the Bodies who travel with me, and the Garage Boys who seem to like me hanging around. They give me licorice, life savers, and Marvel comic books, and tell me I get better looking every day. No one seems to know where Bugsy has gone off to. If they know, they aren't telling. Maybe it's Bugsy's secret. Will Capu and Veloce notice that I'm gone? The Dobermans might think all their friends have left them, too. I'll bring them some bologna when I come back at Thanksgiving. I'll miss watching them playing in the yard. But I'm leaving now. Good-bye Capu, bye Veloce, good-bye empty playhouse, good-bye empty big house. Arrivederci, Uncle Giovanni.

Chapter Thirteen

The Cranbrook School isn't too bad, actually. I'm meeting some new girls who don't know that Gina Mangalli is the niece of Don Salvatore Giovanni. Many of them are so busy trying to impress everyone with their own family history, they don't care much who anyone else is related to. That's fine with me.

I do miss the compound, a little. Mostly I miss my familiar life. But what I miss the most is the ice rink. On Saturdays here in Bloomfield Hills I spend a quarter to ride a city trolley to an ice rink that the hockey team plays on. For another quarter, I skate from nine 'til noon. I go every Saturday. There are no lessons, no coaches, no competitions. And there is no Sandy. I just skate and practice. Some people point at me and kids watch because I'm a good skater. But it just isn't the same. I wonder if Sandy misses me?

I like the teachers at Cranbrook, and I'm doing well academically. I'm learning Latin and algebra. I like geography, biology, and chemistry. English composition is okay, not my favorite; I hate grammar, and diagramming sentences gives me migraines.

In English we're learning to write proper letters. We write business letters, bread and butter letters that say thank you, condolences, and friendship letters. I wrote a nice friendship letter to Sandy. I told her about my school and my dorm room and told her what my ugly uniform looks like. I thought she might laugh about that. I'm sure she's enjoying wearing slacks; everyone's wearing them these days, but not at Cranbrook. I signed it, "With all my love, your best friend, Gina." She hasn't answered my letter.

My favorite class of all is home economics. I'm assigned my own sewing machine. My teacher was surprised that I already know how to thread the Singer sewing machines, and could already sew very well. None of the other girls know how to sew at all. They can't even thread a needle. I want to design a new costume, or make some slacks, but we're hemming tea towels. Mama taught me to hem tea towels ages ago when I was just a little girl.

At the start of the new semester we have a mother-daughter tea. Everyone's mothers come and we all see a film strip together, called "Growing Up and Liking It." Mrs. Scarlo comes with me. As always, she's the most beautiful woman in the room. No one speaks to her, the other mothers just glare at her. She doesn't care. She lights a cigarette with her lighter that looks like a piece of jewelry. She holds her cigarette holder just so and it looks like she kisses it. She wears a pencil skirt that shows off her tiny waist, and jewelry that catches eyes. She has perfect makeup, perfect hair, perfect figure, red nail polish, and high heels. Her stocking seams are always straight and her little hat never falls off. Her gloves always match. She's amazing looking. I feel like last year's scarecrow walking next to her. No one thinks for one minute that we're related. The mothers don't like her. They don't even pretend to. Mrs. Scarlo doesn't care one bit. Neither do I.

So, we all go in to see this film strip. And now I finally understand Mama's obsession with safety pins for emergencies. Well, if anyone thinks I'm going to do *that,* then they can just think again. There will be no Modesses and Kotexes and no safety pins in this skater's tights. That is the most repulsive thing I've ever seen. I know Mrs. Scarlo would never do that, and neither would any skater I know. For sure Sonje Henie would never do that. I can't waste five days every month. What skater could? I'll bet Carol Heiss doesn't waste five days a month. What could Mrs. Scarlo have been thinking? I can't wait to get out of this room. When the lights blink on, all the other girls look as embarrassed as me. The teachers pass out boxes wrapped in plain brown paper, one box for each girl, and a package of safety pins. *I already have a bunch, thanks.* They say we can hide the boxes under our beds – like no one would know what they are. We wander to the big gathering room carrying our plain brown boxes, pretending no one knows what's in them, and pretend to enjoy the tea and cake, while someone plays the grand piano. Mrs. Scarlo whispers real low, "Any questions?" I growl, "Nope." She says, "Good." She seems satisfied that now I know everything about growing up and liking it, and how to use my safety pins. She smuggles me a tiny package. She whispers, "Modern girls don't use safety pins. Put this in your pocket." She winks at me. She smiles at one of the staring mothers who quickly turns away. The very next week I rip the brown wrapper off my box. One more thing I'm not in charge of.

Thanksgiving holiday has come so quickly. My new friend Carolyn, who lives in Bloomfield Hills, has invited me to visit her home, so I phone Mrs. Scarlo and tell her not to send Nick and Vinny until Christmas holiday. Carolyn wants me to meet her brother and go to a hockey game. I'm nervous about being with a different family. I hope no one in that family reads the *Detroit Free Press*. I'm just glad my name isn't Giovanni.

Carolyn's brother Harry plays on his school hockey team so he's a good skater. We talk about skating and he's interested in learning about figure skating. I show him how the pairs skaters hold each other. He wraps his arm all the way around me and my breast rubs against him when I lean into the cross over. I jolt to a stop and he tumbles right over me. He isn't hurt and he and Carolyn are laughing in a fit. I'm glad he thinks it's funny. I'm so embarrassed. *I hope he didn't feel my bra leaning against him. I'm dying.*

"I'm so sorry!" I put my hand over my mouth and pretend to laugh with him. "I, uh, I realized at the last minute that you don't have toe picks on your skates, and you can't do figure skating." *I thought that up pretty fast. I wonder if he felt the bra hooks on my back. That is so embarrasing.*

"Oh, right!" He knocks on his head like a light bulb going off in the comics. "I should have thought of that. Hockey skates don't have toe picks, you're right. You're a good sport to show me, though. Come on, let's just skate around."

Does he really think that? He's probably just saying it to be nice. We skate separately but close for the rest of the afternoon. He reaches out, takes my hand, and we skate around the rink holding hands. I've never done that before. Well, with a coach or a skater working on footwork, of course I've done that. But I mean with a real boy who wants to just hold my hand. I almost forget to swallow. I feel my face warming up even in the cold rink. Carolyn spends most of the time sitting on the benches watching and drinking A & W Root Beers with boys. Skating isn't something she does much, and her ankles hurt.

I hope Carolyn will invite me back again. I wonder if Harry likes me as his sister's friend, or if he likes me for just me, a girl. He's the same age as me, but a year ahead of me in school. Harry goes to Deerfield Boys' Prep. I wonder how it would feel to have my own boyfriend? I wouldn't have to tell Uncle G, or anyone else, about it. It could be my own secret. Secrets are a Giovanni family tradition, after all. I might write Sandy another letter and tell her about Harry. I think Sandy would like Harry. He's not stupid or greasy.

Deanna Klingel

Chapter Fourteen

Christmas Day is always a big deal at the family compound. All the cousins come, all the Staff, Business Associates, lots of people that I don't know who only come on Christmas Day. This year several of the guests mention how much I've grown since Mama's funeral. They'd all been there. I don't remember seeing any of them.

This Christmas Day is different in a lot of ways. First of all, Mama isn't here. She and I always designed and sewed Christmas dresses together. One year we made matching green velvet dresses with detachable white collar and cuffs. Last year we designed tailored red wool suits. This year I'm wearing a grown up dress that Mrs. Scarlo laid out for me. I'm taller, and I fill out the dress bust line just right, now that I'm finally growing. I'm offered antipasto, wine, and treated like a grown up. When we're called in to dine, Uncle G gives me his arm and I'm seated next to him, in Mama's empty chair. With dessert I have coffee and pretend to like it. I hate coffee.

After dinner Uncle G goes to his office, as he always does, and all the visiting families go there, one at a time, secretly. He has gifts for everyone. For the first time, I realize this is another well-kept secret. No one knows what anyone else is given. He'd told me once that gifts should always be given privately because that way the gifts could be what the recipient needed and no one else needed to know or feel jealous, or slighted. I admired him for that, and I thought it was a kind idea that my kind ol' Uncle G thought up from his kind ol' heart.

Today, I realize the gifts are all money. I feel the heat rise in my neck as I take in the significance of that. I'm sure my face is blotchy. In light of all my new knowledge from school, books, and movies, I now have a whole new money vocabulary to work with: money laundering, payoffs, hush money, bribery, skimming, kickbacks, gambling debts, interest, IOU's, insurance. When used in the vernacular of this household, any one of those can be synonymous with *gift*.

I quietly disappear into my room, knowing no one will miss me. From my window I look out on the white lawn and watch the black Dobermans slobbering on bloody turkey necks, hearts, and livers in the fresh snow. I watch the snow turn bloody. Their gift is the only one that isn't a secret. Life was easier when I was younger and questioned nothing. *Who am I? One of the family secrets? Who will I become? Will I always be a mafia princess? Why do I feel ashamed? Who am I? What am I?* I'm a champion figure skater. I'm going to the Olympics. I'm going to travel the world with Holiday on Ice. I'll be in charge of my own life. I will. That's who I am. I can't wait to leave again, I tell the Dobermans.

I spend most of my holiday time at the ice arena practicing

and trying to stay in shape, hoping I'll be able to compete again. I try to see Sandy there, but she never comes. Her coach says she's gone out of town for the holidays. I'm sad, but also a little relieved. I want to remember our friendship how it used to be, and not how it has become. I sent her another letter telling her about Harry and wishing her a nice Christmas, but she didn't reply. What will I say to her if I ever see her again?

It's my last night before going back to school. When I go in for dinner, Uncle G is already at the table. It's set for two: him and me. I'm glad that I took time to dress for dinner and pleased that he wants to be with just me. The telephones aren't on the table and there are no files, no notepads, and no gargoyles; just us. He smiles at me, says the grace, and clears his throat. I know he has something important to say whenever he does that.

"Gina, Baby, how would you feel about finishing high school at a training school for ice skaters? You could go to school and get a diploma, which is what I want you to do, and you could skate, which is what you want to do. How would you feel about that? Sound fair?"

I know how I feel about it, but … "Is there such a place? Where is there a place like that?"

"It's in Colorado. I've had my people checking into it. It seems like a good investment of your talent and energy and my money. That'd be good business for both of us. How about that? It's one of the major figure skating centers in the world, and the most prestigious in the U. S. of A. What do you think?"

Think? I try not to. I hold on to those words, afraid to let them go. I press my hands against my chest, holding the words right there where they're warm and safe and can't be taken back. It sounds like a dream come true. But with my new perspective on our family, I want to ask, 'what's in it for you, Boss?' But I don't. As I've done all my life, I accept my uncle's generosity. I can hardly speak at all. I just stare into his steel blue eyes and marvel at what a handsome, charismatic man he is. He wears his secrets well.

"Uncle G, that sounds like a dream come true."

"After dinner we'll take a look at the correspondence. You'll have a private coach and trainer; the best of everything for Giovanni's god child, huh? Nothing's too good for the niece of Giovanni." He rings a little bell and a staff member brings in two glasses and a sparkling crystal decanter on a silver tray. It looks like a trophy presentation. He laughs and pats my hand. I stare at him. Trying to talk over the lump in my throat is like trying to skate over a crack in the ice – something to avoid because it's dangerous, and the outcome is unpredictable.

I finish out the year at Cranbrook with a really good report card and a few friends, like Carolyn and her brother Harry, who sent me a Valentine card with a candy heart that said BE MINE. I didn't eat it. I wanted to save it for my keepsake, but the ants came in and I had to throw it out. I'll never forget that

I once had it, though. One of the girls saw it and started singing, "Ooo-ooo, Gina's got a boyfriend." I pretended to be blushing and I let them think that.

I come home from Cranbrook in June and in two weeks I'm ready to go to Colorado. I look out my upstairs window at the Dobermans. "I'm leaving," I whisper to them. "And I'm not coming back."

Deanna Klingel

Chapter Fifteen

The Broadmoor Skating Club and Training Facility in Colorado Springs, is as wonderful as the scripts I created for the paper doll plays of my childhood. For the next few years it'll be my home, my school, my family, my world. It's heaven. And I am in charge of me.

Academic School is important because if a student isn't doing well with academics, her ice time gets cut. I study hard, and even get good grades in grammar. Academic School is a means to an end for me. My heart beats on the ice.

I skate every day. I dream my routines. I trace my figures on the steamy shower walls in water beads. I select my music behind closed doors, privately, secretly. I design my costumes on the back of my science project report. I'm immersed in the world I love.

I rarely think about Wyandotte, Michigan, and only occasionally see glimpses of the world news on TV in the student union. I avoid all discussion of current events, always fearful that I might hear something that will crack my smooth existence. I don't talk about my family. I've learned by now, that everyone has a secret or two on ice that doesn't need to be thawed.

Uncle G sends me roses each year on my birthday and he

sent a note to tell me one of the Dobermans had to be put to sleep and that Mrs. Scarlo had died of breast cancer. I read the note, crossed myself, and said a prayer for the soul of Mrs. Scarlo, who had been kind to me in my childhood. I don't feel any real sense of loss. I'm sorry about the Doberman, but I don't know which one had died. Uncle G never called them by name. He always said "the dogs are Bugsy's bailiwick." Bugsy. Whatever happened to dear Bugsy? I must concentrate on this world.

All the great skaters spend time on our ice. David Jenkins comes and goes frequently, Tenley Albright and other past Olympians come to visit and assist the trainers and coaches as guest coaches. Barbara Ann Scott taught for a bit, and a few Soviets came, worked, and left; first they're here, then they're not. It's pure ice skating magic. Other skaters my age like Rhode Lee Michelson from California, come to train, and many others who are expected to become great in the near future. And I'm one of those. I can hardly believe it.

Barbara Ann Scott is amazing and is my newest idol. She's the first North American to win a world title. She did it in Stockholm when she was only eighteen. I'm sixteen and coming on strong. Maybe I'll follow her, who knows? The North Americans are developing a strong team. A lot is going on in the world of figure skating and I'm right here while it's happening. I'll never be able to thank my uncle enough for this opportunity. I owe my life and future to Uncle Giovanni, the man I'm ashamed to be related to. Figure skating is becoming more athletic, and skaters are being recognized as true athletes. The stakes are higher; the bar being raised, and the training is intense. Where will the name Mangalli be in the annals of ice skating history? Freda Rose from the Chicago camp kitchen is working here at the Broadmoor now. She still says I'll be a star. I hope she's right.

I'm really in skaters' paradise. We all dream of spinning like Barbara Ann Scott who's developed a fast-slow-fast-slow spin that is so precise, so finely tuned, that her head never moves, and she spins on one tiny spot on the ice. No one has equaled it, but we're all trying. We all want the strong determination of Tenley Albright who recovered from polio when she was eleven and is an Olympic champion and our heroine. If she can get over polio, I can get over being a mafia princess. Every skater envies the power and strength of Dick Button, the first skater to perform a double axel and triple loop jumps and a flying camel spin. Lots of the boys have groin pulls and knee problems trying to be Dick Button. I skate through my days in a wonderful dreamy mist that someday I, too, will be remembered in figure skating history. I beg my coach for new stuff.

I'm keeping a scrapbook of all the newspaper and magazine pictures and articles about me. I need to know my competition, so I keep track of all of them, too. I hide the articles in my footlocker with the scissors and glue. I don't want anyone to think I'm stuck on myself, or going to my head like Mama warned me about. I just love my life so much, I never want it to end, and I'll have this to remember it all when I'm old. The scrapbook is secret, it's mine, and I'm in charge of it.

One sportswriter wrote that Gina Mangalli has nerves of steel and attacks her programs with the ferocity of a guard dog, and the grace of a snowflake, total fearlessness. Win or lose, he said, Mangalli is cool and composed, showing no emotion. Other girls cry, both happy and sad, but Mangalli is steady. I learned a long time ago that crying doesn't change anything. It only makes your eyes messy. Yep, I just look 'em in the eye, Bugsy.

One magazine has a layout of memorable costumes in films, stage, and sports. The costume I'd worn last spring at the Canadian Open is featured. "Light as an aqua ocean breeze," it says. I hedged when the writer asked who the designer was. I just couldn't say it was me. So I asked to be excused to go to the restroom. When I returned, she went on to the next question. It works every time.

Chapter Sixteen

I got a letter from Carolyn who says her brother Harry is planning to join the army after graduation. Carolyn's going to the University of Michigan in Ann Arbor to become a nurse. She's looking for someone to marry. I wonder how Sandy is enjoying her senior year? She'll probably go to college and find someone to marry. I wonder if she still skates? I've never seen anything about her in competitions or the sports pages. I still miss her. I really do.

I got a boyfriend. Well, sort of. Michael works at the center as a skate tech. He does such a great job on the blades and is in such demand that he often misses his own ice time. During open skate time, I'm just meandering and warming my muscles when he skates up behind me and with his legs stretched out on either side of me, he sort of scoops me up in front of him. He wraps his arms across my abdomen; I stretch my arms to the side and lean back into him. We're skating pairs! What we're really doing is flirting. He smiles like we're performing, and with my head back on his shoulder looking up at him, I smile back. He's so good looking, so close, I feel like I'm melting. We glide around the rink together.

Because it's free skate, the rink organist plays a hodge-podge of music, careful not to play any competitor's program music. So they play a lot of stupid pop stuff. I'm not listening, but Michael is. He spins me out away from him holding one hand, and right there we create a rock and roll dance on ice. We have so much fun skating, dancing, and laughing. We're good together. When the free skate's over, I don't want to leave the ice. I can tell he doesn't want to either. We just stand there balanced motionless on our edges, holding hands, staring into each other's eyes, not saying a word; my heart and time suspended.

Deep inside I hear all my distrust whispering, don't tell me your secrets, Michael. I can't tell you mine. My lonely, empty spot's calling don't leave the ice, Michael. We're good on the ice. My cold hands squeezing his are begging, please don't let go, my eyes entreating, don't ask me any questions. You don't want to know the answers. As long as we're on the ice, we're good together. I don't know how long we stood there like that. But all of a sudden we're both smiling, his hand on my waist, and we're skating off the ice. My hands are shaking too much to untie my boots. I feel an unexplainable frustration with my clumsiness, which must show. Michael slides off the bench to the floor and picks up my foot. He holds my foot up and unties the laces. In times gone by, I would've accused a boy of trying to look up my skirt if he did that. All the girls said they did that, but I've never seen one actually do such a thing. But at this moment, I don't care. I never want him to move. Hold on forever, my boot is calling. He looks directly into my eyes.

"I have to go," he says. "I have class. Same time tomorrow?"

"Yes." I breathe and watch him with his skates tied together over his shoulder, walk out of the arena.

I ask all the girls in the dorm about Michael. No one knows a lot, but I get some fragments. He doesn't board at the center. No one knows where he lives. One thinks his parents live nearby, perhaps he lives at home. Another thinks he has an apartment near the Junior College. Someone says he goes to the local Junior College and works at the center to earn money for ice time. He can't afford a personal trainer or coach, but he takes lessons and everyone agrees he'd be a champion if only he could afford it. No one thinks he has a girlfriend. They've never seen him with a girl, and figures he probably doesn't have time or money for a girl. Or perhaps he doesn't like girls.

"I've heard he's religious," one of them whispered. She made a gagging face. I glared at her. "So?" I sounded angry. She shrugged like a half-way apology. Maybe, I think, I'll have a boyfriend.

Michael and I have become close friends. We spend a lot of time together. We walk into town to see movies. I love the movies. Michael and I often have coffee together at the rink, and I've learned to drink coffee. The truth is, when I'm drinking coffee with Michael, I don't even taste it. We skate, create ice dance steps, and have a great time together. He walks me to the dorm and carries my skate case for me.

For the first time in my life I'm thinking of something other than skating. Michael creeps into my thoughts when I least expect him, catching me off guard and unbalancing me, distracting me. While I draw my figures on the wet shower walls, I feel his arm around my waist. When my thoughts are designing a costume, Michael is wearing a matching male version. I hear his voice in my music, and when my head hits the pillow at night, it's Michael's chest I dream against.

I'm not happy about any of this. I need to concentrate on my long-term goal. Women don't win the Nationals, the World, or the Olympics thinking or dreaming about a boy. Our coaches and trainers have made sure we understand that. I try to concentrate, and I often deliberately avoid seeing Michael at the rink, knowing I'd be "off" in my practice. My legs feel weak just thinking about him.

All we know of each other is what begins and ends on the ice. And that's how I want it to be. If I know who he really is, I might not like him. If he knew who I really am … no, he must never know. I never ask him questions about anything other than skating and he seems satisfied with just knowing my name. The name from Detroit, Michigan, means nothing to the boy from Colorado.

Chapter Seventeen

I need some new clothes. But I still haven't gone shopping or even have much of a clue how to go about it. Some of the girls are lying around on Stephanie Westmoreland's bed looking at fashion magazines. I hang around by the door, and finally muster courage to ask, "Would anyone like to go clothes shopping on Saturday? We could ride the bus into town, have lunch and shop. Any takers?" The girls look at me like I'd just suggested jumping off Pike's Peak. "Just a thought."

I start to walk away, and Stephanie jumps off the bed. "Hey, wait a sec. I think I'm free. Yeah, that'd be nice." She looks at the others and I can see she's trying to raise their support. Gradually, they all join in and we make a plan. I say goodnight and start off to my room already regretting what I'd done. It had to be one of my stupider moments. I cross the hall and stop at the drinking fountain. The girls in the room are chattering and giggling.

"I can't believe it. She invited us? I wonder where she shops. Probably Woolworth's." They all laugh. *Do they think I'm funny?*

"I never knew she went anywhere but to class and the ice." *What's it to them where I go?*

"Maybe she knows of a second hand store?"

"What do you mean?" *Yeah, what do you mean?*

"Has she ever bought one thing new since she's been here?" *They notice what I wear?*

"Really, we should be nice to her. She's really a nice girl. She can't help it if she's poor as a church mouse." *Poor? They think I'm poor?*

"Well, now, wait a minute. How do we know Gina's poor?" *Yeah, how do you know that?*

"Oh, come on, Steph. Haven't you seen her nightgown? Talk about your grannie's gown. She doesn't even have pajamas. Have you ever seen her spend one thin dime? Uh uh. She doesn't go anywhere, doesn't do anything, doesn't buy anything. She obviously hasn't any money." *Or maybe I have everything I want.*

"And she's so clueless. So small town. She's obviously not been anywhere."

"But she's here. This isn't cheap, you know. And where does she get those expensive costumes?"

"Well, la de da, haven't you heard of financial aid or scholarship help? She might not be the brightest bulb in class, but Gina's a top skater. She's numero uno pick for the Nationals. Somebody's willing to sponsor her future, obviously." *Sponsors? Financial aid? Uncle G could buy and sell the bunch of you. Maybe he already has.*

"Well, it could be fun on Saturday. Watching her trying to shop without money will be the best scene yet. We should take her to Philberg's."

"Are you kidding? Even I don't have that much allowance. But it would be fun, wouldn't it?" *Why did I ever think we might be friends? I don't need friends. Well, we'll just see them eat their words. If I learned one thing from Uncle G, it's class.*

In the morning, I stop at the bank on the corner where Mrs. Scarlo has – had – my money transferred each week. I don't know who sends it now – probably one of Uncle G's money men, or his new secretary. They never miss a week but I've never taken any of it out because my school expenses are all paid for directly. I don't even know how much it all costs. And Uncle G doesn't care. But my spending money has just been stacking up at the bank since I've been here. The girls are right. I don't go anywhere or do anything. I take out $800. I'm eager for Saturday. *Well, just you wait!*

We catch the bus after breakfast and ride into Colorado Springs.

"Is this it?" I ask, real snotty like, as we step off the bus. "This is *the* city?" The girls snicker.

"Well, yeah. You probably aren't used to such a big city, huh?"

"Big? Are you kidding? This whole place could fit inside our family compound. Detroit, now there's a city. We have sky scrapers and Hudson's Department Store." *I've been there once.* "We have street cars and restaurants. The restaurant on the top floor of Hudson's has windows all around. You can even see the Detroit River from the skyscrapers." *Or so I've heard.* "Big? Colorado Springs is definitely *not* big, girls." *Okay, they look a little surprised. They've probably never heard me string that many words together. I don't usually have anything to say to them. But today, I can think of plenty.*

We go into the first dress shop we see. They're all oohing and aahing over the ugliest things. They start trying on everything they see. Here comes Jolie out of the dressing room squeezed into a toddler sized blouse and slacks. The girls all tell her how good she looks.

"No," I say. "No. It's all wrong for you. Look." I turn her towards the mirror. She curls her lip a little, but I can tell she likes this ugly thing. "Jolie. It's the wrong size. Besides, ruffles aren't for you."

"I always wear a six. I like things a little form fitting." *Form fitting? Are you kidding? How'd you get this on?*

"No. Jolie. You don't pick out your clothes by the size on the tag. Those sizes aren't *your* sizes, not people sizes, those are the sizes of dress forms. And we are definitely not dress forms." The three mouthy girls quietly study me. *So there.*

Karen comes out with the next ugly outfit the color of a bruise. "Ooh," they all say.

"Not your color, Karen," I say.

"I like this color. How do you know so much about this, Gina?"

"Not a lot of people can wear that shade. And with your skin tone, you have to be careful." All three of them stand there in clothes that look hideous and don't fit, thinking they look so grand.

"Why aren't you trying on any clothes?" *They think I have no money.*

"Because I've yet to see anything I like and that's worth owning. I only buy quality."

"So how come you hardly have any clothes since you know so much, Miss Runway Model."

"Because the private girls' school I went to before I came here required uniforms. And because I'm pretty busy on the ice, in case you haven't noticed, and I don't have a lot of time to waste shopping. Okay? Now, here's the trouble, girls. If you wear your clothes too snug you get dumplings. That never looks good."

"Dumplings?" All three speak at once. *I've got their attention now.*

"Dumplings?"

"What?"

"The good news is that most skaters don't have dumplings. But we do have muscle bulges and that does the same thing to a good line in a garment." They look at each other, scowl, and study themselves in the mirror. *Now I'm rolling. Thanks, Mama.* "You never let the garment define your body, girls. Let your body define the garment. Let it drape naturally. It's a feminine, alluring look, when the fabric is relaxed. Otherwise, it looks like your body is screaming to get out. Too much tension on the fabric is not attractive. I promise you, if you'll go to larger sizes and put on something that actually fits, you'll look thinner, taller, and – no dumplings."

"Where did you learn all this stuff, Gina?" Stephanie asks.

"Don't any of you ever tell that I bought a size ten, do you hear?"

"Jolie, you're so whiny. Who discusses dress sizes anyway?" I ask, like I can't be bothered, which I can't. But I know they do brag about their silly dress sizes. I buy a pair of pajamas, the first I've ever owned, and a pair of gray flannel slacks. The girls say they are expensive, but since I don't know how much slacks or anything else costs, I really don't know. I pretend it doesn't matter. And, it really doesn't. I'm not poor. I tell them I selected the slacks for the fine quality, good construction, and perfect fit. And that's true, I think. They're impressed, I can tell. *How many times have I sat cross-legged in the parlor listening to Mama, Mrs. Scarlo, and the dressmaker talking like this? Usually I wore Mama's pin cushion on my wrist, so I could help. I know so much more than these girls think they do. And more than they think I do.*

"Let's see your dumplin's, Gina," they tease when I slide easily into the slacks.

"Uh-uh. See this? Lots of room. Fabric drapes down from the waist, smoothly over the hips and straight down. A lovely

fit and a nice line. No dumplings. I think they're about a half an
inch too long, though. The cuff needs to rest easier on the top
of my shoe." My body is small, like Mama's, I notice as I look
into the mirror.

"So, you'll roll them up?"

"I'd just roll it up at the waist," Karen said.

I give her my haughtiest, most disbelieving look. "I'm
sure you're joking." They're all looking perplexed, and I feel
very much in charge. I screw up my mouth a little to keep from
smiling.

"One thing, Stephanie. You've got to stand straight. See
how rounded your shoulders are? That'll detract from your
clothes and you won't look as good in your clothes or your
costumes. You need to be as tall and as straight as you can.
There. See? You're so much prettier when you straighten up
those rounded shoulders. Bad posture can destroy the line and
flow of any garment." I yank her up straight in front of the
mirror. *I sound just like Mama and Mrs. Scarlo.*

"Yeah, she's right, Stephanie. It does look better," Jolie
said. *You think I don't know anything besides skating? Poor
little Gina. Now what do you think?* The other two straighten
themselves up in front of the mirror. Everyone just grew an
inch.

"Gina, are you a model or something?" I ignore her. *Let
them guess.* I buy a beautiful cashmere sweater in a dreamy
peach color to wear with the slacks. I buy it at Philberg's and

pretend not to notice them gawking when I pay $200 for it.

We finish lunch, pay our tabs, and all three of them jump up, gather their bags, and head to the exit. "Come on, Gina, what are you doing?"

"I'm figuring the tip. Don't worry; I'll leave enough for the whole table." I tuck a ten-dollar bill under the salt shaker like Uncle G does. He always told me that classy people don't gyp, they tip, and only the cheap, cheat. I learned to tip in Little Sicily on Sundays.

"I never leave a tip. The waitress gets paid after all, why should we tip?" Karen whispered. *Karen, you're a cheapskate.*

"Only boys tip," says Jolie.

"No, that's not right. Anyone who is served and has any class, tips," I say. I buy everyone a black cow before starting for our dorm on the four o'clock bus. In Colorado Springs they're called ice cream sodas, the girls tell me, not black cows. And, of course, I tip the waitress. *I have their attention now.* I'm enjoying this, but I'll never go shopping with them again. They don't know anything about clothes – or me.

Following dinner at the center, like always, I go to my room alone, do my homework, and go to bed. There's a soft rap on my door. I'm surprised, it's Stephanie.

"Hi, Gina. Hope I didn't wake you. Listen, I just wanted to tell you that I had fun with you today, and thanks for all the pointers; I learned a lot. I'm going to work hard on my posture, too. And, uh, I just was thinking, that, well, I've noticed that you always cross yourself before you perform. I do, too. I hope you don't mind that I noticed, but I was just wondering, do you, uh, would you care to go to church with me in the morning?"

"Well, I ... well, I guess so." Stephanie relaxes into a sincere smile. It's the way Sandy used to smile at me. It's not fake.

"Yeah. That'd be really nice, Stephanie, thanks. What time shall I meet you in the lobby?"

As tired as I am, my mind won't let me sleep: *World Championships, Uncle G, coach, concentration, Michael, Stephanie, a friend. Church in the morning. Church. How long has it been?* The thoughts skate in and out of my brain refusing to let me sleep. Life is beginning to feel more normal.

Chapter Eighteen

In between classes I run up the back stairs to my room to switch books. On the way up, I grab the handrail and swing around the corner of the second floor landing, gasp, and nearly drop my books. A man stands there hunkered in his hat and coat. He moves aside and indicates I can pass. With hammering heart, I run up the next landing, still shaking, throw open my room door and seeing someone in my room, let out a scream. Stephanie throws her hand across my mouth.

"Hush," she whispers and kicks the door shut with her foot.

"What are you doing? What is this?" I demand. Stephanie has a big pair of shears in her hand. Sitting in front of her – *who is this?* She faces the wall with a bed sheet thrown over her shoulders covered with clipped hair. On the floor is a heap of dark, curly hair. Stephanie and I have gotten to be pretty good friends since the shopping trip and church, but this ... "Stephanie, this is *my* room, or have you forgotten that?"

"No, I haven't forgotten. That's exactly why we are here. Wait just a sec and I'll explain it. Sit still Irena. We're almost done." She snips away at the girl's hair. It's curly by itself and now that it's short, it's really curly. It doesn't look bad, actually, maybe even cute.

"Irena, this is Gina who I told you about. Gina, this is Irena Vladsoc." Steph is trying my patience.

"We've met. What are you doing in my room? Why are you two here playing barber shop in my room?"

"We're here because you and Irena are exactly the same size, have exactly the same color of hair, and we need help. We need to disguise her. Will you help?"

"Disguise? What for? Well ... maybe ... do what?"

"You probably won't believe this, Gina, but there are men all over this dormitory looking for Irena. They'll seize her, take her back home, and hold her captive in Russia. She's very afraid."

"You mean like the goon that just scared me to death in the back stairwell?"

Steph gasps. "The back stairwell? Oh, no. Really? That's how I thought we'd get her out. Oh, Irena, I don't know what we'll do now."

"Why don't you call the police? Men in a stairwell of our dorm should be arrested, Stephanie."

"We can't. Not yet. Anyway, they'd probably claim diplomatic immunity. Gina, find something casual for Irena to wear. Something no one would notice."

"Stephanie, what is going on here? How can I help if I don't even know what you're up to? Diplomatic immunity? What are you two getting into?" Stephanie moves in front of Irena.

"Irena, can we tell Gina? She won't turn you in, I promise. I know her and she won't." Irena looks sad, but nods a reluctant okay.

"Gina, we've got to get Irena out of the building and into one of the cars parked right at the front door. They'll take her to safety. Irena is defecting."

"De ... defecting? Irena ... have you really thought this through? You know you can never ever go back home again if you do this. You do know that, don't you?" The sad girl nods; she knows that. *And why should that bother me? I did the same thing – defected from Wyandotte.*

"Okay. I'm in. We need a plan." We silently studied each other, then we all began to talk at the same time.

"SSHH. I've got an idea. Irena, get out of the chair. Give me the same haircut, Steph."

"What? Are you sure? Gina, I mean, girl, you've got hair! You've got World Championships—"

"Do it." About half my hair is gone when I start to giggle. I giggle uncontrollably until the whole job is done. I run my hands through the short feathers that curl around my head. I feel so free!

"Steph, you're a genius hair cutter! I love it. Okay. Clothes. Something that would be memorable and stand out."

"Really? You think? I was thinking something to blend in, something that wouldn't be noticeable."

"Nope. Opposite. Let me think." I open a few drawers and

look in the closet. "I got it." I pull on my old Cranbrook gym pants, gray and scarlet, and a bright red corduroy jacket. Just for fun, I pop a red tam over my short haircut. In the pocket of the jacket, I discover last summer's sun glasses.

"Perfect. I'll see you girls in just a few minutes. I'm going down to the lobby to get a drink, case the place, and buy a newspaper. Oh. Do you have any change I can borrow? Irena, I want your bag, too. Take your ID and your passport out of it. Empty it, and give it to me. Lock the door."

I pop out the back stairs and pass the scary guy who looks me over real carefully, while I swing Irena's Baltic folk art design empty bag so he can't miss it. Before I get to the next landing, I hear him speaking into his walkie-talkie. I'm not surprised when a man steps out of the shadows on the next landing. I knew that was coming; that's how it's done. My heart's pounding away, but I smile and pretend I'm Irena trying to be in disguise. When I get to the lobby, I glance around feigning a nervous and flustered appearance. *If I were Irena, what would I do? The girls were right. The place is crawling with Russians. A Soviet Mafiosa? They think they're so clever.* I make a big deal of making myself noticeable, but awkwardly check over my shoulder as if I were afraid I was being noticed. I drop my change on the floor – oops – and let it roll around so everyone would gather to help me pick it up, and notice me, of course. The creeps are watching me and moving slowly toward the door and so am I, trying to look like I don't want to be noticed. I want to check out the cars. Hmm. Black. Of course, black. Cops? Feds? The USFSA? *No one will know; black, Gina Baby, always black.* I know that. I also know what's going to happen as soon as I step outside the door – and I'm right. *One in front, one in back, and one on each side of me. Of course. Gargoyles. That's how it's done.* They put the squeeze on me. I let them grab me good before I shout "Help! Police! Kidnappers!" and everything else I can think of. The campus security is the first one here since they hang around the building. The creeps show their ID and tell the S it's official government business and that I'm trying to defect in this crazy costume. They recognize the bag and know this is Irena, whom they intend to arrest for running away, they explain. "Ve are respons-eeble for her." I take my glasses off. The security looks at me, smiles, and says, "Now, Miss Mangalli, would you do such a thing?" The Russians' eyes bulge out in disbelief. Though I don't speak their language, I know they are blaming each other for their embarrassment. The S winks at me.

"These men have been lurking on the back stairwell of our dorm, officer. They should be arrested." I try to sound indignant, very in charge. I hang around a while, openly accepting sympathy from everyone who saw the incident, and I keep my eyes on the Russians. *How many are there? Where are they stationed?* Finally, I tell the S – loud and clear – that I'm going to my room, but I'll be back soon to go to class, and I'd appreciate it if he makes sure I'm safe from these idiots.

The Russian goons look a little uneasy, doing a lot of sidestepping. I try to look like Wounded Pride and head for the front stairs, walking slow and deliberate. They won't be so quick to move again after that debacle. Goons don't like to be embarrassed. Their boss won't like it. Leave it to a mafia princess to know such things.

I collapse on my bed, take a deep breath, and laugh. "Piece of cake, Irena. Here's how it's done." I send Stephanie down first.

"Look as casual as you can, Steph, don't look at the creeps, just mind your own business, go out the front door, and indicate to the drivers to be ready in two minutes. Got it?" I strip off my gym pants and Irena pulls them on, along with the jacket, tam, sunglasses, her own folk art bag, and we add my book bag, since she's supposedly Gina on her way to class. I pull on a skirt and a cardigan, dab on some heavy makeup and throw my bag, holding Irena's documents and ID, over my shoulder. I snag two Dum Dum suckers and Stephanie's sun glasses, and we happy-go-lucky school girls head out. We walk down the front stairs chatting nonchalantly and casually out the front door. The Russians watch us. I feel their eyes following us. I tell Irena to be friendly, wave and smile at the security the way I would do. I pretend to be one of the snooty girls who never waves. We walk out the door, down the steps, pause like two friends saying "see you later alligator," then I shove Irena into the middle car, throw in my bag, and the cars burst away from the curb, one in front, one in the middle, one in the back. I'm flooded with nostalgia. As I walk away, the sidewalk is crowded with cursing Russians and more cars screeching to a halt then taking off. I pretend not to notice. Newspaper people, never far from the action, begin to appear, sniffing out a story. I disappear behind the building and take the back stairs to my room, and change clothes.

That evening Stephanie's sitting cross-legged on the sofa in the third floor social room watching the news on TV, eating popcorn, and smiling. I slide in and sit on the floor in front of her.

"You're just in time," she says. "Watch what's up next." The news is all about Irena Vlasoc, champion figure skater from USSR, who defected earlier today on American soil. No one knows how she was able to get to the federal authorities and escape the watchful eye of the Soviets protecting her. Stay tuned for a press conference with Federal Judge Stephen Westmoreland. I stare at Stephanie Westmoreland whose chin is resting in her palms. She smiles at the TV.

"Steph. You're incredible." She giggles, shrugs, and straightens her rounded shoulders. I hug her and then I kiss her on both cheeks. She looks stunned.

"Gina, that's so … so European! Where'd you learn that?"

The rest of the school year passes quickly. I spend a lot of time with Stephanie and enjoy having a real friend. Michael and I continue to enjoy each other's company. I try to crowd him out of my thoughts, we dance on the ice, and I try not to be distracted.

Chapter Nineteen

I'm only seventeen and the last week of the fall school term Michael changes the status of our relationship. When I finish my evening ice time and leave to go to my campus apartment, Michael is outside waiting for me.

"Michael! What are you doing out here in the cold? Why aren't you inside?"

"Because you're outside. I only want to be where you are."

He takes a step towards me, wraps his arms around me and kisses me. My legs melt, and I wrap my arms around his neck to hold myself up.

"Come with me," he says breathlessly into my ear.

"Where? Where are we going? It's late and I have ice time at six in the morning."

"This won't take too long. Come on." He has me by the hand and puts me into an old beat up car. *His? Does Michael have a car?* I didn't know that. I hope it has a working heater.

We drive several blocks away from the Broadmoor campus and he parks the car in a numbered space outside a row of cheap town homes.

"Where are we, Michael? What is this place?"

"This is my apartment. Come on in."

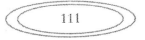

"Michael … I can't go in there. I mean, you know, we just can't … by ourselves, alone? Michael, please understand?"

"This will only take a minute. If you won't come in, then wait right here for me and I'll be right back."

"Okay," I pout. "You know how the press reports every little secret of everybody. I have to protect my reputation, Michael. My coach would kill me if —"

He dashes into the building. I watch him unlock the door and turn the light on. He disappears inside. In a quick moment, he's back, locking the door and running across the parking lot to the car. The car's still running, so he throws it into gear and drives off.

"Now where are we going?"

"I want to show you something. Just hold on. Don't we always have fun together? Well, we're just going to have some more fun." His shirt pocket bulges noticeably. He starts singing "I Want to Walk You Home" in his best Fats Domino impersonation. We often do a fancy footwork routine we made up to this song with its swingy stroll rhythm. Michael and I always have fun together; we have lots of laughs. We don't need to talk much. We know we're good together on ice. We could have skated pairs, but neither of us ever mentioned doing that. It's a huge commitment, being in charge of a pair. I'm just learning to be in charge of me.

Driving along in darkness, I watch the town disappearing behind us. About thirty nerve-racking minutes later, Michael slows the car and turns onto a rough unpaved road on a steep incline. He downshifts and his car complains. The tire spits out some mud and gravel, and heads on up the hill. I'm leaning back in the seat trying not to feel afraid of the car sliding backwards down the slippery mountain and killing both of us. Michael parks the car off the road and we're looking over an entire valley of tiny twinkling lights reflecting on a frozen lake with the moon casting deep shadows all around us. It's a breathtaking sight. I've never seen anything more beautiful.

"Oh, Michael, what is this place? The view is – why are we here? What are we doing here?" I'm suddenly seized with a fear that I know why we're here. The girls had talked about this.

"Michael, no. I can't. Please don't."

"What? Isn't it pretty spectacular? I think it's an amazing sight. I just wanted you to see it. I thought you'd like it."

"Oh. That's it? I mean, it really is an incredible view, and yes, I love seeing it. Thanks for showing me. Can we go now? I have really early ice time tomorrow. You can understand that."

"I do. I'm sorry. I've made a mistake. I didn't mean anything by this, Gina. I just wanted to be alone to ask you something really important and to tell you something important. You don't have to worry. I'm not going to do anything stupid. I'd never hurt you. Don't you trust me?"

"Well, okay then. I'm sorry I said that. What do you want to tell me?"

"Four things really: first of all, I love you. More than anything in the world, I love you. Secondly, I hope that you love me, and I think you do. We've had such great times together; I think you feel the same way. Thirdly, I want to marry you. I want you to be my wife. Fourth, you need to do it right away. I'm going into the army and I'm leaving soon."

I'm stunned. Love? I'd never thought about it. Marriage? We hadn't talked about that. His wife? I'm going to join Holiday on Ice and travel. Now? Right now? I'm going to Philadelphia, then the World Competition in Prague, and then the Olympics. It's all I've dreamed of. Michael is often in my dreams at night. But in the daytime, when I'm in charge of my dreams? No. I don't allow him there.

"Gina, say something."

"No."

He starts the car and pulls out onto the road. He says nothing the entire drive home. I sneak sideways looks at him when cars pass and headlights brighten the inside of the car. His face is shiny and wet. I know he's crying. I find that very annoying.

He pulls up in front of my apartment but doesn't shut off the car, giving me to understand that he isn't walking me to the door. I gather my things and slide to the door. Then I stop. I turn and lean into Michael and kiss him lightly. He kisses me lightly back. And before I know it I drop my bags and my arms are around him and he's leaning over me. His hands are around my head and we're kissing each other. I taste his salty tears between our lips. *Has he noticed that I never cry?* I gather my things again and open the car door.

"Good night, Michael."

He drives off while I stand there in the slush wondering what the heck just happened. That had happened to me one other time. I had taken a really bad fall following an out of control landing of a flip jump. I careened across the ice, bumped my head, and when I sat up I said, "What the heck just happened?" Just like now.

Deanna Klingel

Chapter Twenty

A few weeks later, we're told the rink must close down for a short time. We need to go elsewhere to keep up with our training for the Nationals. The center has acquired a new machine, Zamboni is its name. It's so large that all the entrances to the ice have to be enlarged. The underpinnings of the ice, the engineers say, aren't strong enough to support the compressed weight of the machine, and need to be reinforced. They have to build an annexed garage to park the Zamboni next to the ice. Everyone hopes this Zamboni turns out to be worth all this trouble. Most of the skaters are going home for a visit during the academic break and to train at their home rink. I don't want to go to Wyandotte. I decide to go to Lake Placid, one of my favorite rinks. I'll take some money and get a hotel room near the rink and skate whenever I want. I take all my boots to the tech shop, call the airline, and plan my packing. It feels great to be in charge.

In a couple days, my skates are ready. I go to pick them up and it looks like a new technician with very short hair, his back to me. Then he turns around.

"I hear you're going to Lake Placid. Have fun. And good luck at the Nationals. You're a sure bet for the podium."

"Michael! What happened to your hair?"

He runs his hand over the stubble and grins like he's embarrassed.

"I told you, Gina. I'm in the army. I'll be leaving soon."

"What?" My voice doesn't come out. "When?" I whisper. *Can I still dream at night if Michael is half way around the world?* "Leaving? You're really leaving?" I pick up my skates and walk into the locker room where I sit on the bench and stare at the lockers. Look them in the eye. Michael is leaving. I open my locker, take out my skate case and open it. I look at Sandy's promise. Sandy's gone. My skate case is empty. Michael will be gone. I'm empty. I shiver. I amble like a sleep walker back to the technician's counter.

"Michael," I said. "Yes."

"Huh? What? Oh!" He grins and leaps over the counter, embraces me, laughing. We run laughing out to his car holding hands like we could never let go.

"We need to make some plans," he says breathlessly. "We have to have a wedding real fast."

"A wedding?" I picture weddings I've seen at the Cathedral at Little Sicily.

"Of course. A wedding." I feel numb.

"You need to call your family?"

"My family?"

"Well, yeah. Don't you have a family?"

" Oh, well … do you?" *We've never talked about family.*

"Sure! They're dying to meet you."

"Oh. Oh, that's … that's nice." *They know about me?*

"Well, shouldn't you call them? Where do they live?"

"Yes, yes, I guess I will. Later."

The hard reality settles in. My family isn't just any family. Not like Michael's would be. What if Uncle G said I couldn't be married? Remember what Sandy said? Whatever Don Giovanni says, is how it is. Would I call him? Could I say my family was deceased? Would that be a complete lie? Do I have to tell Uncle G? How would he know? Oh, that's right. He has sources. His people will know.

"The thing is, Gina, my darling, we don't have a lot of time. I'm in the army. We need to do this now!"

"Michael, I'm Catholic."

"Good. Me, too. I want you to come to church with me Sunday."

"Oh, you are? I didn't know that." It seems to me there are a lot of things we don't know about each other. Maybe all we know is that we skate well together. Maybe we shouldn't rush into this. Or maybe I'm afraid not to. I stare into Michael's eyes and for the first time since I was ten years old, I'm afraid.

I call Uncle G. He says he'll take it up with Father Cossini at the Cathedral and I should plan to be married in two weeks on Saturday. He'll make all the arrangements. He asks what Michael does, what kind of money he makes, who his family is. "Do you love the man, Angel Baby?"

I hang up and worry. Do I need to know all that before I

marry him? How much love does one need before it's enough love for marrying? I don't think I know enough about either one of us to commit to being his wife, forever. I don't know who Michael is, but I also don't know who I am. But I can't stand that he's leaving, going away. He wants to be my husband. It would be easier to let him be my husband than it would be to answer all the unanswered questions, wouldn't it? Okay, then, let's just do it. Don't talk about it; don't ask questions, just do it.

The next evening we have dinner with Michael's parents at their home. I've never been in a home like this one, all on one floor. You could almost see all the rooms from the front door. The sidewalk stretches out in front of the home past all the next door neighbors. When you look out the living room window through the lace curtains, you can see into the window in the next house. Not very private at all; perhaps no one in this neighborhood has any secrets. They don't need draperies or gates. Their mail comes right through a slot in the front door. *How do they know the mail's clean if it didn't go through a guard house first?* Their dog lives inside the house. It's a shaggy little dog with freckles. They call it Stubby. Anyone can pet it; it doesn't seem to have a job. Their only car sits in an open carport. *Is it safe? They haven't any security?* It feels unfamiliar and yet – cozy, comfortable.

Michael's mama says to call her Mom. Her name is really Flora. Michael calls his papa Dad. He introduces himself as

Ron, and gives me a little kiss on the forehead. He says he's
always wanted a daughter. I feel terrible. I don't know how to
be a dad's daughter.

There are no bars, no bottles, no little glasses in special
sizes and shapes, no cocktails, no canapés, no little napkins or
olives, and no one to serve them. We go straight through the
living room to a little dining room with yellowing wallpaper
and sit around the table covered in flowered oil cloth. The
Sacred Heart of Jesus picture on the wall is the same one as in
my bedroom in Wyandotte. It's the only familiar thing in this
house. Michael's family reaches around the table and holds
hands while Dad Ron asks the blessing. He thanks God that
Gina is in their family. There is exactly the right number of
chairs: Mom, Dad, Gina, Michael, and his younger brother,
Alan. No empty chairs. Mom Flora, wearing a flowered apron,
goes straight to the kitchen and carries out a pot roast, mashed
potatoes, carrots, navy beans, gravy, and hot applesauce. We
each have one knife, one fork, one spoon, a paper napkin, and a
glass of water. Alan has a plastic Roy Rogers mug full of
Nestle's chocolate milk. There is no staff. We eat hot apple pie
with ice cream for dessert. Mom Flora made it and serves it
herself.

My stomach is full of wormy nerves squirming to get out.
I look around the table and I can see everyone. Only salt,
pepper, and butter are between us; no wine goblets, no big
floral centerpieces or vases, no candelabra, no silver serving

pieces. I can see all their faces; nothing to hide behind. No one else seems to be hiding, either.

They ask a lot of questions about my family and about the wedding plans. I don't know if I lied, if I made up stories, or if I changed the subject. *What did I say?* I excuse myself to go to their little tiny bathroom, always handy for changing the subject, even if it's so small I can hardly turn around without cracking my elbow on something. At the table, little brother Alan tells me about his Sunday School class. Michael just smiles at me. I'm sure I didn't tell them any family secrets. I'm sure their family hasn't any.

After dinner we all go into the living room and squeeze onto the sofa and matching chair. Alan sprawls out on the floor and spreads his baseball cards out for display. Flora and Ron decide to take a walk to work off the apple pie ala mode, and suggest that Alan go with them. The look Dad Ron gives him convinces Alan to leave his baseball cards. Flora winks at Michael. *Cute.*

Michael takes my hand. "I have something for you, Gina. I had this made special for you. I wanted to give it to you that other night when we went to see the stars, remember? Well, I wanted to give it to you then, and I planned to give you a real engagement ring later. But now that we're sort of out of time, and I'm sort of out of money, this all happened so fast, you know, I hope you'll accept this as an engagement gift. Sometime, when we have time and money we can go pick out a nice ring for you. For now, please accept this."

This was the little velvet box I'd seen bulging in his shirt pocket that night. He opens it. I gasp.

"Michael, oh, this is too beautiful! Where did you ... oh, Michael." The sparkling diamonds are set in gold in the shape of our most difficult compulsory figure, so tiny, so artistic, so perfect. The gold chain is so fine it's hardly discernible around my throat. Even Mrs. Scarlo didn't have a necklace this fine, this beautiful, and I'd always admired her jewelry.

"Thank you, Michael. I'd be honored to wear this always and forever as my engagement ring. Thank you. It's truly unique." *Always and forever? Where'd I get that?*

"One of a kind, guaranteed," he says proudly. "My uncle makes custom jewelry in downtown Denver. He chose the diamonds, cut them, and created this to my design. I hope you like it. You know what the design is, right?"

I nod. "Oh, yes, Michael, of course I do." A difficult compulsory figure. Marriage.

It takes my breath away, it really does. Mrs. Scarlo and Mama had taught me a lot about jewelry and I'm sure this is not only unique and one of a kind, it's also very expensive. On the ice, I appreciate the necklace even more, realizing that a ring for a skater is highly impractical. It would really be in the way when grabbing hands or passing through fluttering costume pieces. Skaters don't wear rings. But this ... this could be part of my costume. *Had Michael thought of that? He really is amazing.*

Two weeks later on a Saturday at eleven o'clock, Michael, his family, grandparents, aunts, and uncles that I hadn't met before, fill two rows of pews on the groom's side of the Cathedral in Wyandotte, Michigan. The ladies wear pretty hats, wool suits, and white gloves. Everyone is smiling. Michael's dad wears a sport coat with a bright colored tie. He's sweating and looks anxious, but happy and excited.

The bride's side of the church with the bride's family, which I thought would be Uncle G, and Mrs. Pristas, grew to include Staff, Garage Boys, Pit Crew, the Bodies, cuscinos, "aunts," "uncles," and assorted Business Associates including politicians who were known to me only by their photos. The mayor I recognize, and the director at Willow Run Airport I know quite well. He owed Uncle G a favor and he flew Michael's family here as payback. It was their first trip on an airplane. The pews fill with expensively dressed men and their wives wearing fashionable clothing with lots of gold and sparkling accessories. Their faces hide behind their veils, mantillas, and sun glasses. Michael's family can't keep their eyes off my family. My family doesn't seem to notice them. The gargoyles stand guard at the door, pretending to be ushers, their tuxedos bulging at the hip.

If only I'd had time to think, time to plan. This isn't the wedding of any girl's dream. Because of Uncle G's generosity, and because of the army, the bans and the necessary wait the

Catholic Church imposes, was lifted for us. Uncle G's new secretary Roseanne, Mrs. Scarlo's replacement, purchased the wedding gown and laid it out for me. When I put it on, it fit perfectly, even though it's the first time I've seen it. I'm sure Mama's dressmaker had something to do with that. The long lace veil is beautiful. Roseanne pins it in place and tells me that Uncle Giovanni said to tell me my mother had worn this veil to her wedding, and their own mother had, as well.

I look at myself in the mirror. *My mother had a wedding?* I never knew that. *A grandmother?* No one ever told me about my grandmother. *She wore this?* All I knew is, my father died in Sicily when I was just a baby and then Mama carried me in her arms here to live with her brother, Giovanni. I'd never thought about Mama as a bride. But I know that Mama the designer would say that my necklace is "icing on the cake," meaning it's just perfect.

Chapter Twenty-One

These days are difficult. I really miss Mama. I need to talk to her, to ask her questions. I want to know about my papa. I'd never asked. I want to know if she loved him and I want to know if that mattered. I need to know about being married. Michael insisted that I move out of the training center dorm and into his apartment. My trainer isn't happy with me. Michael says we need to be man and wife; we need time together while we still have it. He says we need our privacy. That part I understand; I've learned about privacy all my life. I'm probably an expert on privacy.

Michael is great. He's kind, gentle, understanding. He prays aloud, holding me in his arms. He says it must be tough to be a girl with no mom. I pretend to not be afraid, but somehow looking him in the eye doesn't seem to be working in my favor any more.

He makes a few comments about my family, and he's beginning to ask questions about them, about my life, about me. I tell him only about me, the skater. I'm hedging, biding my time until he leaves with the army. I'm eager for him to get on the train, and leave my other life alone. But at the same time, I married him because I didn't want him to leave. Did I think that if I married him the army would give him back to me and he could stay at the ice rink forever? I married him, and he's still leaving.

I see a poster of Uncle Sam on a mailbox near the grocery store in our neighborhood. He's pointing at me saying he needs me. I'm so angry I pull it off and rip it into pieces right there on the sidewalk. "You've already got the best part of me," I growl.

I still dream of Michael at night, and now my head really is resting on him. I love how he holds me. I feel so hidden, so protected, wrapped up so tight in his loving cocoon, no one could ever recognize Giovanni's niece. But now, even in the daytime, I can't get Michael out of my mind. My concentration on the ice is shot.

I also need to learn about shopping for food, planning meals, washing and ironing the clothes and making the bed. Michael is totally disbelieving that I don't know how to change a light bulb or how to buy a bar of soap at the grocery store. I hate his crummy little apartment. It has roaches in the cabinets and stains in the commode. The shower doesn't have a drain in the floor just a nasty hole that swallows my Ivory soap bar whole. But I'm pretending to be more happy than frustrated as I learn what it takes to be an important part of someone else's life.

Saying good-bye to Michael at the train station is both sad and a relief. He looks so good in his uniform I want to eat him up. Looking around the platform at all the wives and girlfriends saying good-bye, I realize I'm expected to cry. I don't. I can't.

Michael tells me over and over how much he loves me and he's glad I'm going to be here waiting for him. He says God has blessed him with my love. It's all rather melodramatic. He tells me to put all my energy into skating and time will go quickly and we'll be back together in no time, and maybe start a family. Study hard and get that diploma, he reminds me. *He thinks that's important. Uncle G doesn't.* I don't want him to leave. I want him; need him. But I don't cry. I kiss him good-bye and leave before the train pulls out of the station. I don't think I'm very good at this part of loving. I move back to the training center dormitory that very hour. All the girls now want to hang out in my room. Being married seems to have made me popular.

"Tell us about Michael. What's his favorite color?"

"How was the honeymoon?" They were all giggling.

"When my sister got married she bought everything – even her lingerie – in her husband's favorite color."

"What's he like to eat? Gina, can you cook?" Do you have, uh, romantic dinners? Candlelight? Ooooh." They giggle.

"Get off my bed," I reply.

"What's it like sharing the house with a man?" They all giggle, and gather around me, acting silly.

"Do you shut the bathroom door?"

"Do his feet smell?"

"Do you French kiss with your *husband?*"

"Do you shower at the same time?" They make smoochie noises and gestures.

They want to know all about being married and what married people do. I'm so embarrassed I want to throw up. I'm even rude to them. I've never been rude before, but then, I've never been married before. Now I have something else to be private about; even more secrets. But this time it isn't a shameful secret. It's a personal, beautiful secret. It's about my feelings for Michael and they feel private. I guess it has something to do with love. I don't want to give any of it away. I need all of it. I really want to love Michael – enough. *How much is enough?*

I sit quietly watching the girls taking sips out of their fancy flasks they carry in their expensive bags, secretly, in between their puffs on cigarettes. They giggle and roll around on my bed teasing and asking lewd questions about me and Michael that's none of their business.

"Get off my bed," I holler at them. "Get out and go to someone else's room. You make my room stinky with smoke." They laugh; they just laugh, and wriggle and squirm on my bed, pretending to be making love with my pillows. Sometimes they get so silly they slop their booze on my bedspread. One night I finally give in. I take a sip. I want to laugh, too. Then I take some more sips, and I do laugh. I actually giggle, just like them. And I tell them things that are none of their business. I might even make up some lies. I'm not sure. But we all laugh and sip from their secret flasks. They pass their cigarettes around and I nearly throw up choking. I need to get away. The rink is shutting down for the Zamboni's arrival. I'll go to Lake Placid to train then come back here for the Nationals. I need to concentrate. Get away.

Chapter Twenty-Two

I return from Lake Placid in time to take a couple days off to rest and have some deep massage work. The Nationals are being held at our home rink, the Broadmoor is the host. We are all so excited. Not only does our new Zamboni have a special garage, all the locker rooms have been painted and banners are strung everywhere. We have a new trophy case at the arena and they're building special places for the press and for TV. I stare taking it all in and looking at the shining wet ice, a gift from the Zamboni, when Stephanie runs in.

"Gina, you're back! Wait till you hear the latest. CBS television is coming to the Nationals and the whole thing will be on TV, and Dick Button will be here and he'll announce the whole competition. Can you believe this? We're going to be on "Sunday Sports Spectacular." She's hopping up and down. "We'll be famous on the TV, Gina."

This is beyond exciting. I have to get my concentration back. Some days I feel angry with Michael for coming into my life and stealing my concentration. Other days I'm mad at myself for marrying him. I blame Mama for not preparing me for this and I'm angry with her, too. I've got to get back in charge of my life.

The entire week before the competition Colorado Springs

is crowded with people from everywhere. Hotels are full, the dormitory is crammed. The team doubles up on lockers to allow our "guests" more space. Flags and banners flutter from the light poles. Cars fill every parking place. Snoopy men and women with press cards show up everywhere. Stephanie says one pushy reporter tried to follow her into the locker room where press is not allowed. She slammed the door and broke the woman's pencil!

The day before the opening I double check my ice time to be sure I leave plenty of time. This rehearsal is too important to arrive rushed. I lace up my boots and chop around on the blade covers waiting for my call. When the technician gives me the high sign, I erupt onto the ice with speed and energy. My coach and the press are watching. *Focus, Gina.*

From the center of the ice I can see a large number of spectators in the stands. Everyone in the ice world knows that today is an important rehearsal day for all those hoping to become National champs. I look into the stands and stare them in the eye. I'm not afraid. This is my moment. The music, the ice, they're mine. I breathe deeply and smile a genuine smile. My mind clears. Music bounces off the cold arena wall and I skate. I'm happy with how the boots and costume work, I'm comfortable and relaxed with my split lutz and axel sequence and double salchow. I hold back just a bit today on my layback spin, but this weekend, I'll be all out. The audience responds with cheers and goodwill. Screams of "good luck, Gina" carry

crisply over the cold space above the ice. A reporter is waiting
when I slip my covers over the blades.

"Miss Mangalli, that was incredible," she says
breathlessly. She sounds as if she's just come off the ice after a
two- minute performance herself.

"You were amazing! What do you think your chances are
this weekend? What have you added new to your routine? I
hear your performance costume is pure vision, simply stunning.
Can you tell our readers who your favorite costume designer
is? Do you have any plans to change coaches or techniques?
Will your parents be present tomorrow? Where is your family
staying? We'd like to interview them after the competition.
What would you like to say to your fans?"

I'm pretending to be still catching my breath, while I
ponder her questions. "Please tell my fans that I thank them for
their kindness and their support. If I win this weekend, it will
be for them. Thank you." I take off quickly for the locker room.

I do make the podium at Nationals and the press is very
kind to me. My scrapbook in the footlocker is out of pages. I
am a happily dazed member of the U.S. National Ice Skating
Team. If only I could show Mama my gold medal. I wish
Sandy was next to me on the podium. Uncle G will read about
it in *The Free Press* in the morning. I carry my skate case
around the locker room and ask all the competitors to sign the
inside of the lid. They like that idea so much that everyone else
starts doing the same thing. "Great idea, Gina," they say. *I do*

have some good ideas, sometimes.

We are all given great new skate equipment bags with the new U.S. team logo embroidered on it. Our skate cases are going to be retired. So much for my good idea.

The 1961 North American Championships are next month so now I have to get myself focused on Philadelphia. My coach and I are adding a new element for Philadelphia. I've a month to nail my triple. I've got to get focused. *Concentrate.*

Chapter Twenty-Three

We're packing again. Several of us are going to Philly and feeling very confident. We think our U.S. National Team will cream Canada. We've worked very hard and we're ready as we'll ever be. I got a letter in the mail from Michael. It has a military address with no hint as to where he might be. I don't open it. I can't be thinking of anything but my figures and routine. Nothing else. I shove my clothes into a suitcase, and my equipment into my new bag. I cram my scrapbook and newspaper clippings into my old pink and silver skate case and lock it. *Okay, let's go.*

Philadelphia looks like a nice city. Too bad I don't have time to go sight-seeing. I've been to some really great cities, but I've not seen much of them, as I go from airport to arena to train station to bus station. It would be good to see some of the country, I think. On TV they sing, "See the U-S-A in your Chev-ro-let …" After the Olympics when I go to work with Holiday on Ice, I plan to see some sights. Irena told us she was thrilled to be going to Philadelphia, City of Brotherhood and Freedom. She plans to see the Liberty Bell. "All Americans should," she tells us. Ozal, from Mexico, says the same thing. I think they're right. I'm going to do that. I'm going to see America, one of these days.

My morning performance in the compulsory competition is dismal. I have a shrieking headache that no aspirin relieves. I have Michael on the brain again, and Irena and the Liberty Bell and Alan's baseball cards, and the chairs in Mom Flora's kitchen, the secret flasks, and … and … everything. When I skate off the ice from compulsories my coach is fuming.

"What was *that*?" He's shouting for the entire world to hear. "Any person with eyes could see where your eyes were. Everywhere! Everywhere but on the figures. What were you doing out there? Picking your nose? Gina! Concentration for cripesake. What's going on with you, girl? That was ug-ly!" He follows me to the locker room door still shaking his fist in the air and scolding me. I deserve it. That was my all-time ugliest performance, he's right. I let him down. I let my team down. I let myself down.

Even the judges are annoyed with me and the marks on my afternoon program later on reflect their disappointment in those morning compulsories. That's not fair, but I expected it. They couldn't forget how bad I'd messed up in the morning and it affected their opinion this afternoon.

At dinner I apologize to Coach Yee. "I have a lot on my plate right now."

"Scrape it off."

"I need to take some personal time. I'm not going to fly with the team to the Worlds. I'll meet you there. I'll be there in plenty of time."

"You're already ticketed on that flight."

"I'll pay you back. Nobody needs to know. But I've got to take care of some personal business. Then, I promise, my concentration will be back. Okay? I can get this worked out. Please."

"Get it taken care of. I don't ever want to see that ugly show again. You get your head on straight or you'll be shopping for a new coach. With me, it's all or nothing, Gina. Today was the nothing in that equation. You got that?"

"I do. Thank you so much. I'll get it together, I promise. You'll see the old Gina back."

The team is going to fly from Philadelphia to New York, then Brussels and from there to Prague for the World Championships. They'll take their time and arrive rested. It makes me tired just to think about it. I seem to be tired all the time these days. I go back to my hotel room. I've got a good chance at the podium in Prague. I'm the favorite for the gold, according to several sports writers. I have to take charge of my life again. I have a plan. But first, I'll take a nap, pack, then go see the Liberty Bell.

I fly to Chicago. I go to the arena and talk to one of the managers about Holiday on Ice. I'm surprised that he already knows my name.

"Yeah, I keep track of the careers of all the champs because it's just a matter of time before they burn out of competitions and come in for a real job with real money." I guess he's right. Here I am, looking for fame and fortune.

I don't care about titles anymore. I know I can win anything I set out to win. I am among the best. What can't ever be counted on these days is fair competition judging. The artistry of figure skating is so personal, so subjective. In the international venues, it can even be political. There's no definitive way to score jumps, spins, salchows, lutzes, camels. It's all in the point of view of the judges, and they, like everyone else, have personal favorite every things: jumps, costumes, countries, people. I've been over this and over this. So what's the point? We skate because we love to skate. We love to perform. We love to excite the crowds. We love our costumes, the drama, the pageantry on the ice. We risk injury and give up our other lives. So what's wrong with being paid? I audition and sign a contract that very day. I'm in charge of my own life.

I've never needed money, never handled money, never even thought about money. I have a stack of it in the bank. Now, I suddenly want to earn some for myself. I want to handle and smell my own money. I'm not sure what I'll do with it when I have it. I'll need to buy a wallet to put it in. Maybe I'll buy a Chevrolet to see the U.S.A.

The producer, the director, and two arena managers smoke cigars and look over the contract. The smoke makes me nauseous, but I tough it out. I agree to start right after the World Championships, when I return from Prague.

"Gina Mangalli," the producer says, studying the name and chewing the stub of his cigar. "You're about to become famous."

"Four weeks," the director says. "Rehearsal for this season begins in four weeks. Monday, 10 A.M. Don't be two minutes late. Five minutes late, we dock pay."

"I'm always the first one on the ice," I assure my new boss. "And, I'm the last to leave."

He winks at me. So, he's not the tough guy he pretends to be, cigar or not. Back at O'Hare I buy a *Philadelphia Inquirer* at the newsstand.

Summary of the 1961 North American Figure Skating Championships

One of the biggest surprises and disappointments of the skating competition yesterday came when Olympic hopeful Gina Mangalli, representing Broadmoor and a member of the U.S. National team, failed to medal after a disastrous compulsory performance. Mangalli, well known for her fearless attack of her programs, intense concentration, stunning costumes and showmanship seemed strangely detached with a complete lack of focus. Even her sporty new hair style, which her fans adore, didn't help. She seemed ready to make up the difference with an outstanding program, which fans felt were given unnecessarily low marks. Dick Button, in his commentary, wondered why her very minor mistake was so costly, when the overall program was outstanding. After receiving the devastating marks Mangalli was interviewed by Tom Brookheiser of WCAU and Jack Whitaker, formally of Philly station WCAU, now with CBS Sports, who asked her about her disappointing performance. Her reply was, "My congratulations to the skaters on the podium. They deserve to be there. I wish everyone a safe trip and the best of luck for the World Championships two weeks from now in Prague. We'll all be there as a team, and we'll all give it our best. I apologize for my performance today." Steve Fox of the New York Times has noted that Mangalli is not only the top female skater in the U.S., she is also very classy. Young skaters everywhere are adopting the new free spirited hairstyle of Gina Mangalli. Mangalli has also instituted the new tradition of a special handshake among the competitors to show their team unity. She's a crowd favorite."

Classy, huh? *Classy is a family trait, right? Uncle G would be proud.* I fly to Detroit, feeling smug now that I have a money secret of my own. I'm eighteen, on my way to a World Championship, and I have a real job. I'm a professional ice skater.

Uncle G seems really happy and surprised to see me. He hugs me, laughs, and wipes his face with his handkerchief. He takes me into his inner office where I've never been before. *Had Mama ever been in here?* He pours me a drink from his bar and seems to expect me to drink it. I've never had a drink of his bourbon; I'm sure it's better than the girls have, which I don't like. I watch him at the bar. It's a man-sized piece of furniture. The polished mahogany reflects the sparkle of the cut crystal decanters and the assortment of crystal glasses. It looks like a trophy case.

I take the glass and sit down in the leather, king-sized chair. I know full well that the Bodies are just outside the doors, timing my audience with their boss, and the S's are making sure we don't get interrupted. I sit the glass down on the little table beside me and stare at it. Uncle G catches on right away.

"Drink it slow, Gina. That's the secret. Drink it slow. You're old enough to drink, but let Uncle G give you some advice, Darlin'. Drink it slow. Never empty the glass. Then when someone wants to refill it, you can say no thanks because you still have some. Moderation, Gina. It's all about moderation, good manners, and class. It's not classy to be drunk. Never let anyone see you soused. You've never seen anyone drunk in my house. I don't tolerate it. Too much drink dulls the business mind. We have to keep our edge. Let your opponent get iced, but you drink slow. Got that?" I nod. "Good. Bottoms up."

We salute each other's glasses like the Business Associates do. I pretend to sip, but I hate the smell and the taste of the golden liquid.

"You'll get used to it," Uncle G assures me. Uncle Giovanni and I talk for more than one hour in his inner office.

I've never had an audience with him that lasted that long, ever in my entire life. It's nice to see how interested and concerned he is for me and my life. He tops off his drink several times. And although he never empties his glass, he empties the bottle. His eyes are a little glassy, but he – he is classy.

He asks me, "How's married life?" I shrug, feeling my face blush. *Why does everyone ask these personal questions?*

He asks about my skating career. He's supportive of my plan to join Holiday on Ice. I don't tell him I already have.

He asks about Michael, where he is, does he write, is he good to me? Did I need anything? Money? Did I want a car? He'd like to buy me a car – for a wedding present, he says. He asks how close I am to a diploma. I figure I'm within a semester. He says not to worry, I'm married, so it doesn't really matter anymore. "Know what that's called, Gina? It's an M. R. S. Degree. Get it?" He laughs a silly laugh and wipes his perspiring brow. *I don't think Michael agrees with Uncle G about that.*

He wants to have a party to show off the skating star of the future, new blushing bride, his favorite niece, all that kind of stuff. I agree; a party could be fun.

A rap on the door interrupts us. I'm surprised it hasn't happened sooner, but I'm delighted that it hasn't. Uncle G checks his watch and stands up. For all that family visiting, I've almost forgotten that I'm talking to a crime boss; a criminal who loves me and a business man whose audiences are timed. I didn't get to ask him my important question – the real reason I came back.

I walk around in my stone and tile play yard. The fountain still sprays, but looks green and slimy from neglect. The playhouse has bird droppings on the mossy roof. Two dusty little chairs are still empty. If things had been different, maybe Sandy could have sat in one of them. I watch old Capu romping with his replacement Doberman buddy, Tauru, the bull. Tauru eyes me suspiciously and I know better than to approach. I pull a couple chunks of ring bologna out of a waxed paper wad and hurl them over the wall into the grassy yard. I hear snarling and slobbering.

Up in my old room, I look through my closet of secret stuff. My worn, torn paper dolls are still here; my little diary with the key that Mama gave me. It has only one entry. It says Dear Secret Friend Diary, and I wrote Diary all about my first big competition. I hadn't known enough secrets to fill any more pages. There are a few old snapshots I'd taken with my Brownie camera. I wish I had a picture of Sandy and me. I used to have a picture of me taken by the gate, but I gave it to Michael. Everything I have here is from skating. I guess it's been my whole life. It's who I am. There's nothing else here. I shove it all into a pillow case.

I stand by the door to Mama's room a long time before

finally going inside. Where are her things? I wouldn't begin to know. Where did she keep her letters, her mail, her pretty fountain pen, her silver thimble? Did she ever keep scrapbooks, or photos? Did she have my baby picture or my birth certificate? How about her citizenship papers? Was she a citizen? I never asked. And now it's too late. Was my grandmother still alive when Mama came here? Had she ever seen me? Did she ever hold me? Did Mama guard her secrets, or did she not have any?

I sit down on Mama's old chenille bedspread. "How old were you, Mama, when you got married? Were you scared that night? Did you like being a wife? What was my father's name? What did he look like? Was he kind to you?" I lie back on Mama's pillow and try to breathe in the scent that was Mama. But the closed room is dusty and smells like moth balls.

I open the closet door and see several cardboard boxes stacked there. "How many secrets did you keep, Mama? Did you know any of your brother's secrets? How many secrets do we need? Did you love him, Mama? Were you going to tell me all this? Were you going to tell me how much love a wife should have? When I get ready to step onto the ice, Mama, I cross myself and I pray for you. Do you know that? I don't want to forget you. I told in confession that I'm so sorry I let you get sick. I know if I'd been here you wouldn't have gotten polio and died. But now I'm telling it to you, Mama. I'm sorry;

I'm so sorry. I'm trying to make my life good, so you'll be proud of me. When I'm on the ice – I'm good – very good."

After dinner I ask Uncle G where Mama's sewing machine is and if I might have it. He says that can be arranged. Her rosary was buried with her. I don't think she had anything else. Uncle G says I should have her mink coat.

"Mink coat? Mama had a mink coat?" I'm incredulous. Mama never went anywhere.

"Look in her cedar chest or in her closet."

Mama had a mink coat? What else don't I know about Mama?

Chapter Twenty-Four

Roseanne laid out a red dress for me to wear to the party. I hate it. Mama and Mrs. Scarlo had much better taste. Roseanne smells like cheap perfume and her clothes are all too tight. Doesn't she know that smooth, draped lines and well-fitting garments are much more flattering? Doesn't everyone know that? I don't care. This will be the last dress that someone else selects and purchases for me. In a few weeks I'll have my own earned money in my new wallet and I'll buy my own. I'll be in charge of my own life.

I wear the red dress with matching red sandals to the party. I make sure my nylon's seams are straight, and admire my diamond necklace, which makes the rest of the outfit look classier. Mama has ruby earrings in her jewelry box; I borrow them. I'd never seen her wear them. I remember Mama with her tiny pearls piercing her ears. Did she ever wear anything in this big jewelry box?

If Uncle G had seen the leers I got from the Garage Boys, they'd have been in deep stew. One of them, Dirk, whistles, draws in his breath and whispers, but I hear what he says. I frown at him. "I won't tell your Boss you said that." He rolls his shoulders and looks sheepish. "I 'preciate that, Miss Giovanni."

"Mangalli!" I shout. "I'm Gina Mangalli."

"Right! Sorry." He knows better. That's his way of changing the subject when he doesn't like how the conversation is going. Me? I just go to the restroom. Dirk? He messes with people's names. That always changes the conversation. He probably doesn't know that I know he does that. He thinks it's one of his clever little secrets. One thing that's not a secret here in the compound is how Uncle G feels about using bad language and swearing. One time when I was young, I heard him giving one of the boys a tongue lashing. He said, "Educated gentlemens like us has good vocabularies. We got lots of words we can use. We don't need no swear words. That's cheap dirt. It's sinful; it's vulgar. It ain't done here. We don't say the Lord's name in vain. Got that?" He slapped the pit's head. "Don't let me hear no cusswords coming out of that garage again. That clear?"

I think that's pretty clear. Clear as ice. Sometimes, though, when there's a sudden climate change, ice gets foggy. But the fact is, growing up I never heard any bad language around the compound. Here in the compound, there's no drunks and no blasphemers. Just extortionists and gangsters.

I'm treated like a grown up at the party. I'm offered the oysters, drinks, and olives. Sober men with clean mouths, who are probably criminals, ask me to dance. One said I'm a real good dancer. *Am I?* I tell him I'm a skater. That's probably the only thing about me that I know for sure.

I wonder two things at the party. One, am I grown up now because I'm married, or did I get married because I'm grown up? Two, since I am married, should I be dancing with these other men while my husband is in the army, or should I dance with these men because my husband is in the army? I don't remember if I'd ever seen Mama dance with a man other than Uncle Giovanni, her brother.

The next morning Uncle G presents me with a Ferrari. He says he remembers that I like red cars. I was planning to buy a car for myself with my own money. But since I know nothing about buying cars, or even how to drive one, this is probably a better idea. The Garage Boys and the Bodies teach me to drive around the compound. They take out some black cars and we all drive together in the yard and the driveways so I can get the hang of driving in traffic. I look the little car in the eye and take it on. I almost run it up the maple tree nearest the driveway, before I get the feel of it.

All the Staff seems really bogged down in work and very edgy these days. Uncle G's in his inner office with the phones and the bar, in his outer office with his Staff and Roseanne, in the parlor with other men, some I've known all my life, some strangers. He wipes his face with his handkerchief. I eat alone. Everything is behind closed doors, even more secretive. The S's hunker around the compound. It's quiet except for the phones ringing, answered by Uncle G's muffled voice. Worry lines age his handsome face. There's a tenseness in the air that's noticeable even in this place where tense is normal. A car full of newspaper reporters turns up at the gate. Weasel turns the dogs out and raises the Chicago Piano in their direction. I see cameras poking out the car windows. Weasel shoots their tire out. A lot of activity, but it doesn't include me. I want to ask Uncle G what's going on, but I rarely see him. Tiptoeing around, I pretend I'm not here. As far as everyone else is concerned, I'm not. I need to talk to Uncle G – alone. It's important; it's the only reason I came back. And then I'll leave for Prague. This time, I'm really not coming back. I pace in the hall outside his office.

I finally catch Uncle Giovanni alone in the dining room reading a stack of morning newspapers underlining things and making notes, drinking his Bloody Marys with one of the telephones tucked into his neck.

"Gina, good morning. Come in, come in."

"May I speak to you Uncle G?"

"Of course, Gina, come on in here. Want anything? You eat breakfast yet? Bloody Mary?" He looked at his watch.

"How can you drink something called a Bloody Mary and not feel like a cannibal?" I asked. He laughed.

I nod that I had eaten, but I hadn't. My stomach is queasy, and talking about bloody anything was churning it more.

"I wanted to ask you for a favor, Uncle G."

"Of course, Gina. You can always count on me, eh? Whatever you want, name it!"

"Could you help me get my marriage annulled?"

"What has he done to you," the words rumble out of a deep throat like the distant thunder of an approaching storm. "If he's done one thing, I'll—"

"No. It's not that. It's me. I'm just not ready. I'm too young. It was all such a mistake: a hurried, unplanned mistake. I need out. I don't want to be married. Not yet."

"You're reneging? That's not honorable. You vowed, that's an oath. You know better than this. Your word is your honor. Our family is honorable. Marriage is for better or worse. It's forever, a sacrament. It's sacrilegious to think this way. Let me pour you a drink. You need a drink. Bad business, Gina. Bad Business. Have a drink."

He gets up and moves to the cabinet that holds the hidden bar of the dining room and pours me something that I don't want. He refills his own. "Drink it," he tells me. "It'll clear your brains." The smell nauseates me.

"Uncle G, I've joined the Holiday on Ice. I'm going to travel and make my own money. I don't want to be married. It'll be two years, maybe more, before Michael gets back here to be my husband. Then we can see if we really should be married. I don't even know what his favorite color is." I know I sound whiny, but I can't help it. I'm desperate and I really am his little girl; his favorite niece. I guess I'm begging.

"His favorite color? Who cares? Maybe he's color blind."

"I just mean, I don't know him, not really."

"Two years should give you plenty of time to get to know him."

What happened to "Whatever you want, Angel Baby?" I guess he doesn't call me that anymore – now that I'm someone's wife. He said no.

I went up to Mama's room. I find the mink coat. Mama really did have a mink coat. *What else did she have that I knew nothing about?* I open the first cardboard box in the closet; then the next; and another. There are seven cardboard boxes with empty Vodka bottles sealed inside. *I didn't know Mama drank Vodka.* So, Mama did have secrets after all.

A packet of documents lay in her top drawer, with her expired passport on the top of her lovely lingerie. Something ties itself in a knot in my stomach. I should know what's in this packet. But now, I'm not sure that I really want to know. Would it change anything? Would I have to change my memories of Mama? I lean lightly against the drawer and allow it to gently close.

I pack my things, and box up Mama's sewing machine. I find her little spools of silk thread and shove them into my suitcase with my silk stockings. I put her silver thimble on my finger; it's a perfect fit. I drop it into my pocket. I keep the ruby earrings. I zip the mink coat back into its bag, hang it up, and close the closet door on all the secrets. I'm leaving. I'm never coming back. Grownups can't live in an empty playhouse. I'm headed for Prague to meet the team, then to the ice arena in Chicago where I'll live happily ever after, in charge of my own life. The Pit Crew helps me load my things into my little red car.

"Big mistake, Gina Babe. You shoulda got a Brinks insteada this little tin can. It ain't big enough for all this crapola."

I laugh with them. "I never knew I owned this much stuff. You're right, it's mostly crapola."

Behind me, several yards away, I can hear Capu whining. He wants to say good-bye. I decide to name my car Veloce, in honor of his old friend. It looks like it's going fast when it's standing still; fast, veloce. I look around at the family compound and realize I'd never referred to it as "my home." No wonder I don't mind leaving it. Arrivederce, Capu. I sigh deeply, and open the car door myself. I reach inside and pick up my new wallet with my new driver's license tucked safely inside. I really am all grown up, and I really am on my own now. I can't wait to get started. Finally, I'm in charge of my own life. The glorious afternoon sun is dropping behind the trees. The deep shadows look like black mantilla lace. A soft breeze rattles the leaves. The fragrance of the gardenias wafts on that breeze. I suck in a final lungful of my past as the air around me explodes.

Deanna Klingel

Chapter Twenty-Five

The Dobermans erupt into a raucous fit. The guard house and Weasel blow into a million pieces. Chunks of stone, cement, and iron rain down through the trees and bounce off the red tile roofs. It doesn't even take a second. The explosion resounds, echoes, and stops in my ears. Everything else happens in a muted silence, in slow motion. An exploding tree limb spears across the yard. The Garage Boys sprint, yell, guns in front of them explode destruction as they run. The Staff shoves through the door and everyone shout orders that no one hears. My play yard tiles shatter and collapse; windows blow out; gardens and fountains disappear, water shoots in all directions. Cars race through the space where the gate used to be, and rapid gun fire zigzags through the blue smoky air in the compound yard. Uncle G is in the doorway waving his arms and shouting, "Gina, Gina, now! Get down! Take cover…" I stand there frozen against my new red car. My day-old driver's license in a new empty wallet is in my hand covering my head.

Cars skid and swerve all over the yard spewing grass and gunfire. Uncle G disappears; machine gun fire ratchets all around me. One end of the garage roof blows off, gargoyles shatter, and oily smoke billows into the sky. Nick grabs me and hauls me through the smoke and debris up the marble stairs, taking two steps at a time, his knees beating against my ribs. Bullets zing off the pillars of the porch. My leg rips out from under me. *Where did it go? I can't feel it.* Nick is on top of me, burying me. My head cracks hard on the marble floor of the porch. Nick's body completely covers me. When I open my eyes, I peer into the wide-open, steel blue eyes of Uncle Giovanni. Through spittle bubbles he whispers, "Gina … Baby…"

The dogs are still howling. When I look over at them, the guardhouse is gone and the iron gate with the big gold G is bent out of shape and gapes wide open like a big yawning mouth that has lost its teeth. The dogs can get out now if they want, but they aren't trying. They're just spinning around yowling. They hover over something, or someone. Bodies lay around in strange contorted ways, missing some of their parts. The air is clouded with dust and debris. One of the cars has smashed into a tree, and hissing steam squeezes through the folded hood. The driver hangs over the front fender. Thick black smoke roils out of the garage. My new car is polka dotted; the windshield shattered. I take in all this mess in just a moment's time, like one big panoramic mural on a restaurant wall in Little Sicily. Nick is struggling to get up and there's blood all over the place. It's mine.

Chapter Twenty-Six

I'm not sure how many days I've been at Saint Michael the Archangel Regional Hospital Center. Long enough to be tired of having other people tell me when to eat, when to sleep, and when I need to go to the bathroom. I don't eat, I sleep a lot, and talk to no one. Finally, one of the nurses, who's probably as sick of me as I am of her, comes in with an orderly and the two of them plop me down in a wheelchair.

"We're going visiting," she says gruffly. In the hall next to my door, sitting in a chair was a Fed. *What's he doing here?* He nods at the nurse and gets up. She pushes me into the elevator, and then down a hall. The Fed follows us. There at the end of the hall sit two Feds. She pushes me into the room between them where Uncle G lies in bed. He isn't in very good shape. In fact, he looks like he might be dead. But he isn't; not yet, anyway. We hold hands, and he tries to talk through a little neck plug that isn't working too well. The nurses, all nuns, hover around him. One tells him that the priest is coming to hear his confession before lunch and his attorneys will arrive after lunch to be sure his will is in order. I look around, but the gargoyles are nowhere to be seen.

Uncle G struggles with his neck plug and tries to make jokes. "They treatin' you okay? Nothing's too good for

Giovanni's niece, remember that. Gina Baby, tell them I don't eat baby food, eh? I can't eat anymore of this baby food. I need a good Chicago steak."

The nuns shake their heads and throw up their hands playfully, like they can't do a thing with this man. And they probably can't. There's no bar, bottles, ice, or glasses in this room, no telephones, no secretary, no newspapers, no cigars, no racing forms, no gargoyles, no Bodies. How on earth can Uncle Giovanni survive in a place like this? We hold hands for a little while. I don't say anything. What's there to say? He falls asleep and the nurse takes me back to my own room.

I'm not sure how I can survive here, either. The nurse's aide brings me ice water each morning. I pick out the ice, hold it in my hand, and pet it while it melts. I have to get out of here. I write a long overdue letter to Michael:

Dear Michael, I've had time to think about this, and I'm sure you aren't surprised to hear that I cannot be your wife. It was never right from the start. I was immature, naïve, and selfish. I still am. I'm on thin ice. But I have got to try to make sense out of my existence, and I need to do that before I can be anyone's wife. I need to take charge of my own life. When the annulment paper arrives, please just sign it and forget that we were ever married. Come back from the army and find a mature woman who wants to be your wife and live happily ever after. I'll never forget the fun we had together, but I will try to forget that we made a terrible mistake marrying in a big hurry.

I sign with all my love, which will never be enough. Gina.

I don't include a return address. I don't have one. I also don't have any annulment paper, but I plan to get one, somehow. I don't cry, not exactly. But I feel crummy. When I was little and pulled a mean trick on one of the Dobermans or on any of the Garage Boys, Bugsy said I was a turd. That's what I feel like for what I'm doing to Michael. Is my life just one big lie, one big smelly turd? Is that all it's ever been? It's just a whole new set of lies and secrets; a fresh turd.

When I finally have a visitor, it's someone I don't know. He's tall, broad, good looking, wearing a trench coat, holding his fedora in his hand. He's friendly and polite. He says his name is Doug Fairlane. He already knows my name. In fact, he knows a lot about me.

"Have we met before?" I ask him. *Where have I seen you?* "I think my pain medication is making me a little forgetful or foggy." *Is that really my voice?* I haven't spoken to anyone for weeks. I haven't had anything to say, really.

He says he's watched me almost all my life, though he isn't an ice skating fan. The only time we'd met face to face was in Chicago at the train station in 1957 when I was fourteen.

"We weren't supposed to meet yet, it just worked out that way." *Oh, now, I remember: tall man. Badge. Sandy and me. Best friends forever.*

"I knew we were destined to meet sooner or later," he says. "I wish it'd been sooner rather than later. My plan was to meet up with you in Chicago. I know you were going there to work. I'm sure I'm not the only one who knew that. I was hoping to bring you in then, before they got to you. I'm sorry you got hurt badly before I got to you."

What's he talking about?

Fairlane is full of information. I didn't know that Uncle Giovanni is soon to be indicted. It doesn't matter now, he'll probably die anyway. All the people who've ever cared for me, protected me, taught me, are dead or soon to be, indicted or already in prison. Most of the Giovanni Family Secrets are being exposed in Senate hearings and appearing in the headlines in every paper across the nation. I'm learning just how large and bent my family tree really is; it's decayed from the inside out.

"A secret starts with a little fib; just a little nick in life's smooth surface. Then it starts to grow, like a crack in the ice. When it reaches a certain size, it takes on strength, a width of its own. It's harder and harder to conceal it, and before you know it, it creeps all the way to the very edges of its existence, determined to show itself to the world. Like a crack in the ice when it gets too big to be safely contained, the secret, the lie, becomes dangerous." The slurred words poured out of my mouth. *Where did that come from?*

Fairlane looked at me oddly. "You're quite a philosopher, Miss Mangalli. They said you wouldn't talk to me. They say you haven't spoken since you've been here. Guess you been saving up. A bit of a poet in you, huh?"

I glanced at the clock on the wall. It's almost time for my pain medication. I ask Fairlane to mail my letter to Michael. He says he will. He pulls a newspaper out of his deep trench coat pocket and lays it on the bed. *Do all cops and crooks wear those rain coats with big pockets?* He leaves and I spread the paper out over my cast to have something to do. *February 15th? What is today's date? This paper is several weeks old.*

February 15, 1961. Brussels – Oh! Oh no, what's that date? I struggle to sit up straight and clear my eyes. *HEADLINES. HEADLINES.* Dear God! NOOOO!

Seventy three people, including 18 members of the U.S. figure skating team, were killed this morning when the Sabena Airlines, Boeing 707, crashed on its approach to the Brussels airport. The team was enroute to Czechoslovakia, where the World Championships will open next week in Prague. Among the passengers were coaches, family members of the team, U.S. skating officials, and most of the U.S. figure skating team. All on board, and a farmer on the ground, died.

In my ears it sounds like another ambulance siren. But it's a scream from deep within my soul piercing my heart and wrenching its way through the tunnel of my throat. Nurses and orderlies on soft silent shoes fly into my room like vultures on road kill. A nun with a needle. I wail and flail hearing only muffled sounds: Metallic clinking of the window blinds. Someone closes them. Water splashing over a basin. Someone rinses the bed pan. Someone flushes. Cabinet doors thump shut. The wastebasket scrapes on the floor, the dumped refuse clatters, the basket replaced in the corner clinks on the linoleum. Strips of sunlight squeeze between Venetian blind slats and fall across the bed. Call buttons chirp for attention at the nurses' station where chattering indicates shift changes. Ice rattles in the fresh water pitcher. How can life go on? How can white shoes walk up and down the halls squishing like dry sponges? How can water flow and work continue, shifts change? How can the sun shine? How can the hours continue to change? How can dead skaters skate? Life is over. The world must be as quiet as me. It has nothing more to say. Give it a pain killer. But there aren't enough pills in the entire world to dull a pain like this. *I should have been there, too.*

Chapter Twenty-Seven

I have several months of rehabilitation to manage before I can even begin to think about how my life has melted down. My left leg is broken and is in a cast. My right leg has been shot up real bad. I begged them to cut it off. I don't want it. It hurts and makes moving too hard. Just cut it off, just take it and be done with it. I hate the ugly, deformed, mangled leg and I don't want it to be mine. I'm angry with the know-it-all doctors who say I can learn to walk again. Walk? Who cares about walking? I have to skate. Why do I care if the leg is left there to dangle uselessly? A cripple is a cripple with or without the damaged limb. Just like my old Sonja paper doll, I'll never stand up by myself again.

"Take it off," I scream at them over and over. "This leg will never go to the Olympics and it won't be skating with Holiday on Ice. I don't want it. Take it off!"

During the second month of rehabilitation my next worse nightmare is confirmed. I'm pregnant. I am furious. Who was supposed to tell me about these things? My Mama? She never told me I could get pregnant if I didn't want a baby. No one did. What about all those smiling couples in magazines with their cute little babies? Sure, I know how they made the baby. I had life science class in school. But I thought it was because they *wanted* to make a baby. I didn't know it could be a surprise made on your wedding night if you didn't even want one. I am really sick and tired of other people making my life's plans and decisions for me. When do I get to be in charge of my own life? When?

Now I have a leg I don't want, and a baby I don't want. And I have to keep them both and learn how to live with both. I have a wallet that's empty and I'll never skate for Holiday on Ice. I have a new driver's license that I'll never need. I don't have a car, or a leg to drive one. I'm buried alive in grief and guilt. My life has been run over by a Zamboni; I'm a puddle on the ice. I'm no one.

The New Plan for my life, just like all the other plans in my life, isn't being made by me. This time it'll be made by the FBI. The plan's called Witness Protection. They're guaranteeing me a safe, protected life, in return for all I know and the identification of some pictures. I had thought my entire life had been safe and protected. I'm seeing now that it was only isolated.

The information and identifications Fairlane wants has to do with the family secrets. I'm sure that I don't know the secrets. I only know they were there, hidden in the crystal decanters in the secret bars, in the cardboard boxes in Mama's closet, in the garage, in the locked boxful of license plates and magnets, in black cars, in the safe in the inner office, in the recorders in the telephones, in the guard house, in the ammunitions cabinets guarded by Dobermans. I'd grown up surrounded by secrets without ever really knowing what they were. Fairlane says there are mobsters who think I know more than I do. I'm not safe, he says. Since I don't seem to have any other plan, I agree to witness protection. Gina Mangalli is dead.

I'm able to identify many of the photos Fairlane shows me. I give him the names as I know them, and he confirms them with their real names. I squirm when he tells me what their jobs are. Many of them were regular visitors to the family compound, some are members of other families, some are clients, some were really my family. I feel sick to my stomach for days as I learn more and more about our family businesses, our visitors, and the clients I'm identifying.

I learn that organized crime in Little Sicily, the leader being my uncle, involves extorting grocers and merchants who buy protection from the mob. They control liquor sales, gambling, horse racing, prostitution, labor unions, and politics. They even control "law enforcement."

"What?" I gasped. "Law enforcement?"

"Exactly," Fairlane replies with disgust.

Fairlane tells me that the mob has a complicated hierarchical organization, and rules that they all obey.

"Rules? Crooks have rules? That's funny, Fairlane."

"Right." He chuckles. "Honor among thieves, that sort of thing. Rule numero uno: Family is definitely off limits. That's why we weren't looking for this attack at your home. The mobsters are firm about that point. Homes and families are sacred and kept out of the action. They really surprised us when they broke that rule." *I never remembered calling the compound my home. Maybe that's why the mob thought it was okay to attack there.*

"Rule Two: they are all silent about mob business. It doesn't surprise me that you don't know much about any of this that was going on around you all your life. The fewer people that know mob business, the safer for all of them." *Get Henson on the phone down at the Free Press. Remind him of my rules about this family.* I nod. "Uh huh." *Mama, why can't Sandy come to my house to play?* "Yeah, I get that."

"Conspicuous consumption of alcohol is also a rule. Perhaps you noticed how *inconspicuous* that was, hidden bars, that sort of thing. Public drunkenness is low class according to the mafia rules." *No drunken bums in this family, Angel Baby. It ain't classy.*

Fairlane smirks a little at the irony of the mafia's social rules. I've been smirking for a few years now, too.

"Journalists and politicians cannot be killed. Nice, huh? Their murders would draw too much newspaper attention. The mob has reasons for all their rules." *The mayor, the governor, the newspaper editors, were all at Mama's funeral and my wedding.*

"Yeah, nice."

"There's another rule, too, that goes unspoken: no offense

goes unavenged. It's their *omertà*, their code of manliness.
They consider themselves men of honor, who all belong to
Onorata Cocreta."

I'm stunned. Men of Honor? Who blow each other to bits
over some breach of etiquette ages ago? Uncle Giovanni is ... a
man of honor? My head pounds and I can feel sweat beads
forming under my bangs, and in my armpits. *Yeah, he's a
classy man of honor.*

My broken ribs are aching under their tight wrap where I
can't scratch or stop the dripping perspiration. My good leg is
elevated in a cast. My lost leg is hanging wherever they laid it;
right now, I don't care where that is. My concussion gives me
headaches beyond tolerable, and I gulp the pills as soon as I
can have them. Fairlane comes and goes out of my
consciousness.

On the first page of the pictures, I only recognize one
picture. "This is Frankie Fingers. He came to Uncle G's
birthday party in Little Sicily and brought him a pretend cake
that a girl jumped out of. I was maybe ten at the time. I've seen
him several times since."

"His name is Frank Coppola. Have you seen him more
recently?"

"I haven't seen anyone recently. I wasn't there,
remember? I've been away at school and training."

"Convenient," Fairlane says. "I have to hand it to your
uncle. That was a convenient plan."

"Convenient? I thought it was because – "

Of course. It's convenient. What's left of my heart splits wide open. My face stings, like a huge slap.

"Just do the best you can here, Gina. Try to stay awake. Coppola deals in smuggling, Detroit to San Diego. He doesn't live around here, works out of Toledo, but he's been in touch a lot lately. Fingers might have had a finger in all this. We're piecing it together. Toledo's not that far. We think Coppola wanted more of the Detroit action. We've been in on that for a while."

On the second page, I know nearly everyone. "This is Uncle Pete, Jack, and this older man is Papa John Parelli. Papa John speaks mostly Sicilian. His English isn't very good. This man's name is Joe and this is his son Tony. They've visited us from Toledo before and stayed over, many times. Tony brought me a bubble pipe with a tube of gooey bubble stuff when I was a kid. He's only a few years older than me."

"Very good. Tony Parelli you say? This one here? Toledo? You sure?" He nods to his partner who writes in his notebook, checks it against the number on the picture, and leaves the room. "I'm on it," he says.

"This nasty looking one here? I hate this man. He really does look this nasty. The Garage Boys make fun of him. They call him Screech, because he has a really screechy high voice. He acts real creepy, and when he's around, Uncle G doesn't want me near him. The Garage Boys told me that too. They said, "When you see this nasty sucker coming, Gina Doll, you get the heck out of his way. He ever touches you, honey, we'll kill him before your uncle even tells us to.'"

"Yeh, that all makes sense, Gina. The mob doesn't hold with his kind. He's an ex-con. Busted for pedophilia in Port Huron. A real pervert. He's trying to find a family to support him, but I don't think any of them want him. The mob doesn't like his kind. Too unreliable, for one thing. He's a small time loser and couldn't afford a gig this big."

"That must be why Uncle G told Mama one time that Screech would tarnish the family reputation."

"That would be the story. You're doing fine, Gina. Do you need to rest a bit? I'll go get a coffee and you take a little nap. I'll be around when you wake up."

Sounds good to me and I close my eyes and take relief from my pills. The third page later that day puts my stomach in spasms. "This is Uncle G." Fairlane nods.

"Trunk of the family tree. Yes. Salvatore Giavonni."

"Weasel. Nick. This is Vinny, he came later. They were my Bodies."

"Body guards," Fairlane sums up for his partner. "Pretty clean, except for the company they keep. Weasel is Wesley Iannacone. This would be Nick Scarlo. And Vincent Dial, a young twerp."

"Scarlo? Did you say Nick ... Scarlo?"

"Mean something to you?"

"Nick? And Mrs. Scarlo? He's her son? I never saw them being – you know, like a mama or a family." I'm shocked. I'd never even asked him, Nick what? How could I not have known?

"Bett Scarlo? Right. Her husband was killed in the line of duty – so to speak, on an errand in Vegas for Giovanni. Left her and a little boy. Giovanni's been looking after them ever since, as part of his family."

"She was Uncle G's secretary." *So, that's why Nick used to go to school in the garage.* "Uncle G was fond of Nick. But I never …" I sigh. I'm so tired. "These guys here are all body guards. I'm not sure of all their names. I always called them the Gargoyles. But not to their faces, of course." Fairlane gets a kick out of that and chuckles.

"I like that; we need to add that to their rap sheets: Gargoyles of the first degree." He laughs again.

Bugsy used to tell me he liked my sense of humor. I wipe my brow. My headache is making me nauseated.

"Ever hear of Stephano? Milazzo?"

"Yes. I think, Gaspar Milazzo. But I'm not sure which one he is. Stephano? Stephano … maybe Magaddino? Maybe. Yes, I think that's it. But just names I may have heard. I don't really know them. This one – I've seen him quite a bit, but I don't think I ever knew his name."

"Good. You're doing great, Gina. Ever hear of Lucky Luciano? Vito Genovese?" I shake my head. I'm not much help. "Did your uncle ever do business with anyone in Las Vegas?"

"Yes. He brought me a present from there once. A scarf."

"Ever hear the name Bugsy Siegl?"

"Yes. Yes, I remember another Bugsy. There were two."

He smiles and writes a note on his yellow notepad.

"Okay, how about the cuscinos who went to your school?" He turns the page.

"In the garage?"

"Yes."

"Well, I'm not sure I really know any real names. I recognize their faces, though. Each tutor kept his own class; we didn't take roll or anything like that, not like at regular school. But I knew Randy, Squirt, and Wiener. These three right here. They're brothers – they were teenagers, actually – a few years older than me. They finished school and I haven't seen them since."

Fairlane writes it down. "Sounds like Singing Sam's boys, all right. They're in custody for some stupid street action. Singing Sam is fit to be tied. We're waiting for him to do something stupid himself. Like father like sons."

"This one ... this is Bugsy. I don't know his name, just Bugsy." I feel drained looking at his photo.

"Really? You don't know his name?"

I shake my head. "He was always real good to me and the

Dobermans. He was kind of – like a friend. I, uh, didn't have many, you know. He went missing when I was fifteen. I asked, but no one knows where he went."

"He was in charge of the security of your compound. Did you know that?"

I nod. I feel like a traitor to Bugsy, but I don't really know enough about him to do him any real damage. *Bugsy liked Boston Baked Beans candies.*

"Bugsy took care of the dogs. And the mail. And anything else that came or went through the gate." I'm feeling worse by the minute. "He had this … gun. The Chicago Piano … it was part of his job."

"And a whole lot more: explosives, surveillance, wire taps, arsenals. Bugsy's fingers were into a lot of dirty business. His name's Robert Mangalli."

My throbbing head jerks up. "Mangalli?" I whisper the name that gets caught in my throat. It tastes like poison.

"Yep, your father's brother – your uncle. I take it you … didn't know that?"

I feel dizzy and lay back, dropping my aching head against the pillow, letting the nausea pass. My broken good leg is throbbing. The other one doesn't care.

"Where … where did he go? He's been gone a while. No one said. Is he—"

"No, no he's not dead. At least, not yet. Bugsy turned himself in. He did it for you, Gina. He saw this mafia war heating up. He had a lot of inside information. He knew there was vengeance involved. Something big was going to go down, he just didn't know when. You were the most vulnerable and he was sure they'd come for you, send your feet and hands in a nice gift box to Giovanni, something cute like that. Bugsy really cared about you. He turned himself in, by Jove. Said his job was to provide security. The only way he could provide security for you, was offer state's evidence in return for a reduced sentence, but mostly for the assurance of your safety. So, we traded Bugsy for me. I was supposed to be looking after you. Sorry I didn't move in fast enough. He'll probably be killed in prison before he's paroled. But he knew that going in; it's a given. The mob's effective on both sides of the cell walls. Bugsy's been involved in some pretty bad stuff. He's top of the list for a lot of kingpins. They'll get their vengeance. But meanwhile, he's your hero, Gina."

I shiver and shake inside my skin, which feels like it's melting off my cold bones. I start to sag; then I throw up.

"Whoa, there, girl!" Fairlane jumps to my side. He props me up and yells for a nurse.

"I know this isn't easy, Gina, but it's important. You've got to hold it together, okay?"

"Yeah, okay." I take a breath, lean back again, and shut my eyes. The nurses come to clean me up and send Fairlane packing.

In another month I will leave this ugly place with my

useless leg, empty wallet, driverless driver license, and meet my new godfather, Doug Fairlane of the FBI, who knows more about who I am and who I was than I ever knew. We'll meet at some unknown secret place. Only ghosts reside at the family compound, what's left of it; it's now under lockdown by the Federal Government. They tell me the garage went up like an atom bomb and shattered windows outside the compound. I don't want to see it. I'll never go back. I ask Doug Fairlane to get Mama's sewing machine and my pink and silver skate case from the wrecked red car, and he says he will. Gina Mangalli is disappearing into a hole in the ice with all the family secrets, never to be heard from again. Only Doug Fairlane knows who she will become, and where she's going.

Chapter Twenty-Eight

The inside of the safe house looks as ordinary as the restaurant on the corner near the Training Center in Colorado Springs. There's nothing memorable about it; innocuous, like a black car. You could walk past it every day to buy a newspaper and never recall seeing it.

But I have to remember everything I hear in it. I'm learning my new identity. I'm no longer the niece of Don Salvatore Giovanni. I have a new family history. I'm not Mama's daughter, though my new mother is also deceased. I have a new social security number; I never knew I had an old one. I have to learn my new mailing address. It looks like I live in a post office box. I have to memorize my new existence, a new personal history, with more details than I'd ever known about my real history. And I have to learn to maneuver in this wheel chair. I'm determined to get out of it. If Mama had lived she'd be living in one of these. I think Mama's lucky.

I can't tell Michael I can't be a wife because I can't walk or skate or drive a car. I can't tell him that we made a baby by accident on our wedding night. I can't tell him my family is dead or in prison. I can't tell him I have a new life. I can't even tell him who I am. He's not a part of this life. In his life, Gina Mangalli died in an airplane crash.

Marian Starr lives quietly in a three bedroom cottage near Tacoma, Washington. My address is a post office box. I live on the bus line and it's a short ride to the A&P Grocery store, the drugstore, a fabric store, a liquor store, the bank, the post office, and the library. The whole town. What else do I need? I have a telephone, I bought a radio, and subscribed to a newspaper. I plan to be better informed in my new life. One bedroom is mine, one bedroom is for the baby, and the third is my sewing room. I have no plans to sew anything, but I need a place for Mama's sewing machine. I'm Marian Starr. Freda Rose was right after all; I did become a Starr.

Every month, money from the estate of Salvatore Giovanni, what's left of it, inheritance from Carmen Vittori Maria Giovanni Mangalli, and another untraceable deposit all enter my new bank account by certified bank check from a Swiss bank account. All my money from Colorado Springs has found me. I have no idea how any of this money stuff works, it's a mystery. Fairlane promises me this is all legal and no one will ever know where my money comes from. The bank will see it as a return on Marian Starr's successful investments. I take money out in cash because I've never learned to use checks and I'm too embarrassed to ask the banker to show me. I'm sure he'd wonder where I'd grown up that I missed out on all that. Uncle G always paid in cash. He said checks got messy. I don't want messy.

I walk with a leg brace and crutches and live with chronic

pain. The black boot of the leg brace takes twice as long to lace up as my skate boots ever did and is a lot more uncomfortable. It's the ugliest thing I've ever seen. It's the iron lung for the leg. Thank goodness the drugstore is close by and my doctor is generous with pain medication. Every day the pain is a constant reminder of the past I've sworn to forget. *Time for another pain pill and a drink; don't worry, Uncle G, I never empty the glass.* How can I forget my past when I'm dragging it around in this brace?

The bank pays my bills, I order groceries, read the local paper, listen to the radio. I don't go out or do anything. The leg hurts, and it makes me angry. It's so ugly, so useless. I, too, am ugly and useless, and I can't always remember my new name. And I'm mad...very, very mad. Sometimes I get so mad I throw something. I used to be good – so very good – on the ice. Now, I'm nothing. Nobody.

Shortly after "Marian Starr" settled in Tacoma, Washington I ride the city bus to the hospital where everyone admires my courage. The sympathetic nursing staff is aware that Seaman Randall Starr, my made-up lie of a husband, is in the U.S. Navy, and they happily take a picture of our infant, Sienna Starr, to send to her daddy, a great American hero, who, of course, will never return. I'm so used to a lifetime of secrets and lies, what does one more matter? I might be tempted to tell the truth, but I'm not sure what it is.

I'm a whole new person, with a whole new set of secrets.

Some nights I look out the window and it's all dark. Just me and Sienna are the only people awake. I've hired a nurses' aid to come by each day to help with Sienna. I don't know what to do with a baby, what they need or how to take care of them. I'm afraid I might drop her. Or maybe I'm afraid I'll contaminate her. I'm not fit to be a mother.

I name the baby Sienna because Fairlane told me Mama was originally from Sienna, Italy. I learned from Fairlane that she went to Sicily to marry Stefano Mangalli, the don of a huge, strong mafia family there. He sent his brother-in-law, Salvatore Giovanni, to the States to set up his business there. Giovanni spoke good English and was very smart. Stephano Mangalli, my wealthy father, was assassinated, butchered in his own vineyard, Fairlane said. And then his widow, Mama, came here to be cared for by her brother. So, I thought it would be nice if the baby could have some connection to a real person. That, of course, will have to be another family secret.

Sienna is the first newborn I've ever held and she terrifies me. I've seen them at baptisms, but I've never held one, or touched that wrinkly fragile skin. It's creepy. The nurse says that isn't an unusual reaction, and I will learn to love her. How does something that little and helpless have the power to terrify me? I stare at her long eyelashes. Look it in the eye, I tell myself. I wonder how much love I need to have for her. Will I ever have enough? How does someone *learn* how to love? Did Mama learn to love me? Could I have learned to love Michael?

Stop. Fairlane warned me I cannot revisit the past. Michael? Who's he? Marian doesn't know any Michael. Marian doesn't know anyone.

I stare into her small eyes, the same steel blue color of Salvatore Giovanni's eyes. Her nose is a miniature of Michael's. Her curly black hair is like mine and Mama's. She cries a lot. How can I keep from visiting that past? It's going to live and grow under my roof. Look her in the eyes and don't be afraid. I think of the Dobermans. I wonder what became of them?

PART TWO

SIENNA

Deanna Klingel

Chapter Twenty-Nine

I bought her a red plaid school bag from the fall Sears Roebuck Catalog. We laid out her school clothes before she went to bed. Sienna tossed and turned most of the night. She starts kindergarten today and she was too nervous to sleep. She's wearing a red cardigan sweater and new red T-strap sandals, a yellow raincoat with a hood and yellow rubber rain boots. We write her name on the insides of each boot and in the neck of the raincoat: Sienna Starr. She's wearing one of the two new dresses I sewed for her. We buy Crayolas at the drug store. I fill out all her registration forms and put them in her school bag. She's had a smallpox vaccination, can go to the restroom by herself, and can count to ten. Her stuttering is worse this morning. This will be a hard day for her. She's shy, I suppose because she doesn't see many people. I will start sending her to catechism at the church so she can see other people, maybe get over her shyness. She walks two blocks and gets on bus number seven, just as we practiced. I know her heart is pounding. Mine is too, as I watch her walk to the corner. Always I wonder, who else might be watching?

"How was school?"

"O-okay."

"Just okay? You don't look too happy about it."

"My teacher says Sienna is a s-strange name. Is that b-bad?"

"It's not. Don't stammer."

"I'm s-sorry. One of the boys said I was a b-baby."

"You sucking your thumb?"

"I'm s-sorry, Mom. I didn't mean to. D-don't be mad. I won't d-do it anymore."

What do I know about raising a daughter? I don't know anything normal kids do. Is she normal?

"Can we make some new paper d-dolls today, Mom? I'll make one for my friend P-p-patsy, too. I told her we make them from the Sears Roebuck Catalog. She said she never heard of making paper d-dolls. She's nice, Mom. She t- talks to me."

"Tell you what, kiddo. We'll make something special for your paper doll today." I cut out a tall model in a bathing suit, glue it to cereal box cardboard, and trim around the woman's figure. Sienna cuts out the clothes, carefully adding tabs to wrap around the doll's shoulders. I draw a pair of ice skates on the back of an envelope and cut them out, leaving tabs on the sides and bottoms.

"Here you are, now your paper doll is an ice skater."

"A ice-k-kater?"

"An ice skater."

"What will she d-do?"

"Just this." I turn on the radio and skate and dance the doll across the table to the music. "She's skating."

Sienna smiles, takes the paper doll, and continues the long program with the paper doll.

What am I doing? I can't go there. Stupidly I've opened a can of worms. I'm angry with myself. I limp off to my room and shut the door.

Sienna runs to my door and calls to me. "M-mommy I'm s-so s-sorry. I didn't mean to be s-selfish. You can have a t-turn. D-don't be mad."

My head aches; I need a pain pill. I open the closet and look up to the top shelf at the pink and silver metal case. My life. On a shelf. I hear Sienna sobbing on the other side of the door.

SIENNA

I wonder where my classmates live. Sometimes one invites me to come to her house to play. I don't go because I'm too shy and because I know Mom would say no. I ask if I can invite a friend to my house. Mom says no, kids give her a headache, she says. She's had a headache since I was born. It's my fault. I cried a lot, she says. And I stutter and I suck my thumb. When it isn't raining, I sit on the front step and toss bread crumbs to the squirrels. When it's raining, I play paper dolls in my room. I'm sorry I don't really know what she should look like skating because I've never seen an ice skater. I wish I could skate.

Patsy Freeman feels sorry for me because the rest of the class is mad at me and she says it isn't really my fault. The PTA plans an ice cream party for any class that has 100 percent attendance of parents at the PTA meeting. In our class, everyone's parents came to the PTA meeting except mine. So our class doesn't get an extra recess with an ice cream party. Patsy Freeman says it isn't my fault because we're only kids and we can't tell our parents what to do. She sees me crying on the playground, feels sad for me, and invites me to go ice skating with her. Mom doesn't want me to go; she says I won't like it, and it's dangerous. I beg and cry and promise I won't ask for another thing for a whole year, and she finally throws up her hands and says okay, I can go. That was so lucky! I'm so excited.

Patsy's sister loans me her outgrown ice skates. I love the smooth feel of the ice, the wind blowing on my face. More fun than I ever had. I want to tell Mom how much fun this is, but it might give her a headache. Patsy's big sister can skate really well and she says I'm a natural at it. Patsy's mother thought I already had ice skating lessons. Lessons? Ice skating lessons? There's ice skating lessons? I break my promise as soon as I get home and start begging.

Mom orders my ice skates from the Sears Roebuck Catalog, and uses the telephone to arrange my skating lessons at Lakewood Winter Club here in Tacoma. At my first lesson, I already know. I want to skate forever.

Deanna Klingel

Chapter Thirty

MARIAN

I hate it when she's away from me. Yet, when she's with me, I can't think of a thing to say to her. The only thing I know are the things I can't talk about. I practice what I'll say when the day comes that she asks me about her father. I'm so tired of living like this. When I can't stand it anymore, I take a pill, take a drink, pull the drapes, and go to sleep.

Fairlane says he knows I'm on the hit list for at least four mafia members still at large with wide connections. Why? Because their family needs revenge against the Giovanni family for something lost in generations of mafia history. Maybe because they think I could identify them. Do they have any idea how clueless I was all those years? They think I might know something or have heard something. I guess they don't know that I didn't have access to any secrets. Fairlane finally gets that. He says it's in my favor that most people think I died in the plane crash with the other skaters. He's not convinced that the mafia all believe it.

"We're keeping tabs on them. We'll know if they start to get warm." I close the drapes.

Sienna really likes going to the ice rink with her friends. What would it be like to feel the cold on my face, to hear the blades slicing the ice again? It's a life I have to forget. She can go play for now. I'm not encouraging her. It might help her self-confidence. She'll outgrow it and go on to other things. For now, I wonder if I'm jealous. I worked so hard, only to have it yanked away. She'll make her own life with her own dreams. I hate to be the one to tell her that dreams don't come true.

Meantime, I pay for the best coach around, Kathy Casey, who, luckily, is right here in town. I'll let Sienna play as long as she wants. But it'll soon become serious work. Then she'll give it up and go on to other things like most young skaters. I wonder where Sandy is?

I'm really proud of Sienna. She's working at school and at the rink. I know what it takes to get those podium positions and still keep up the grades. I see her practicing her balance, positions, and movements in the yard. I can see she's graceful, and my heart breaks.

I was good; I was the best. I worked hard. I had dreams. I deserved a chance. I can't even show her my scrapbooks. Gina Mangalli, ice skating star, Olympic hopeful, died with the others. There is nothing left of me to share with her. I'm no one. I'm a paper doll.

I'd love to make Sienna a costume, but a homemade costume would only embarrass her.

Chapter Thirty-One

SIENNA

"Mom, Mom, you'll never believe this: I qualified. I have my third podium position. I qualified and I'm going to the Regionals. I can't believe it. I'm s-so excited."

"That's nice."

That's all she says. The most exciting day of my life and all she says is *"that's nice."* I've worked so hard for all these years, and she says, "That's nice." Actually, I should be glad she's awake to say anything. Usually when I come home from school or the rink she's passed out drooling over the sofa pillow. She says she doesn't sleep well at night. Or she says she works nights and has to sleep in the day. She doesn't work. Sometimes her story is she has a migraine headache. They started the day I was born. I don't ask anymore. One time last year, in eighth grade, I had high academic honors and made the honor roll, plus I had perfect attendance. I ran all the way from three bus stops back to tell her. She was annoyed that I woke her up just to tell her that. I don't tell her much at all anymore. I'm sorry I ruin her day, her life: I'm sorry I'm her headache.

She doesn't understand anything that goes on at a skating rink. How could she? I try not to be boastful or anything like that, I just want to tell her how much fun it is, and how good I can skate. I've competed a lot and done very well. I'm not so shy anymore. Our rink has an annual "Showboat," like a dance recital on ice. But Mom has never seen me skate. I guess people who haven't skated or don't know anything about skating aren't that interested. So I try not to bother her about it. She's never come to the rink. That hurts my feelings, I guess. I've stopped asking her.

I think Mom grew up poor. Seems like maybe she's not very educated or worldly about things. She's sensitive to questions about her life, so I don't ask. When I ask a question it always turns into Mom yelling and me crying. It's always my fault. I beg her to forgive me; I don't know if she does. I spend more and more time at the rink. Sometimes I even do my homework at the rink. Then I feel guilty; I should be here to help her. I wonder what she does all day? What did she do before I was born and gave her a headache?

Chapter Thirty-Two

"What are you sewing, Mom?"

"Pajamas."

"Let me see? Oh, neat! Can you make me a pair, too?"

"You want me to make you pajamas?"

"Sure, why not? You used to make my clothes when I was younger and I had the prettiest dresses in class. Remember that gorgeous Easter dress you made for me?"

"Okay. Pajamas it is. What color?"

"What are my choices?"

"Looks like red plaid or redder plaid." Mom laughs aloud. It's the first time in a very long time I've heard it and it sounds so strange; so special. I love the sound of her laughter, something I rarely ever hear.

"Know what I'd really like, Mom?" She looks up from her sewing machine and looks directly in my eyes. It's been a long time, I think, since we've looked into each other's eyes like this. I'm afraid I'm treading on thin ice. But I foolishly skate on in.

"I'd really like it if you could make my costume for the Regionals; something really unusual and pretty." She turns off the lamp, leaves her sewing, goes into her room, and slams the door behind her.

"Mom? Mommy? Are you okay? I'm sorry. I really am. Forget it, okay?" I speak to the door, as I often do, but it doesn't answer. I did it again. I always ruin everything. "I'm sorry, Mom." I'm talking to the door – again.

I order my costume from the catalog like everyone else. We try to pick out unique ones, but they all look fairly similar. I try it on, and like everyone else I use safety pins to shorten straps, tighten waists, scissors to shorten the skirts, and glue to reattach loose sequins. I don't show it to Mom. It looks awful.

The week before the competition I come home to find a costume lying on my bed. It's like a butterfly, no, like a breath of air, gossamer. It's so beautiful, it takes my breath away. And what's this? Matching covers for the skates? Oh!

Mom is in her sewing room; I can hear the whir of the wheel and the rhythm of the foot treadle. I know better than to disturb her. Besides, I know the door is locked. I put the costume on. It fits like new skin. It's perfect. Under the arms she's made tiny pleats so I can raise my arms over my head and the costume never shifts up. *How did she know to do that?* The skirt is slit, like the petals of a daisy, so when my legs move they're completely free. The color is … I don't know. It seems to be every color imaginable, like auora borealis. I stand in front of the mirror. *Mom must have gone a long time without a drink or a pain pill; she must have stayed awake a long time; she must not have had a migraine. How long did it take her to make this?* The door opens and she nearly walks right into me.

"Mom, this costume is amazing. Thank you so much!" I reach out, grab her, and hug her. *When was the last time I did that?* I feel her body stiffen, then relax. She puts her arms around me. It feels so right. She smells like cigarettes.

"Mom, are you okay? You feel okay?"

"I'm fine. Why are you always asking me, 'Mom, are you okay?'" She says it in a sarcastic little baby voice.

"I'm sorry, Mom. I didn't know I always asked that. I didn't know it annoyed you. Sorry. Thank you for this, it's fantastic." Mom loses her balance, sways, and then stands up.

"I'm sorry." I start back to my room.

"Come back here. Tha's rude, Sienna. Do your homework right here. I need some comp'ny."

"Yeah, sure, Mom." I know she's been drinking.

"I need another pain pill."

"When was your last one?"

"So who you think you are, Flornz Nightingale? I can read prescriptions; I don't need a teenage nurse to tell me when to take my meds, okay?"

"Sure. Sorry, Mom." Her words are slurred; there's no point in talking. I sit at the table and stare at my algebra book. My tears are dropping onto the pages. Many of my textbook pages look like they've been left in the rain. I no longer pray for her.

When the team at the rink sees my costume they're speechless. Everyone wants to know where I got it; it looks nothing like the catalog selections.

"Stunning," Coach Kathy says.

"My mother made it," I tell them proudly. A couple of jealous girls make snide remarks, but most of them are just dazzled. Some ask if she contracted.

"Have we met your mother, Sienna?" Coach asks.

"How much does she charge? Does she have samples?" the skaters want to know.

I fix supper that night to be sure we sit at the table together. Mom starts to complain about her headache coming on. I quickly move her to the table to smell the Campbell's Tomato Soup, her favorite. When she's busy slurping her soup, I begin my rehearsed speech.

"Mom, several of the kids at the rink would like to order their costumes from you. I was thinking that if I took on more of the housework, you'd have more time to sew. You enjoy sewing and you're so good at it, and you'd make some money besides. What do you think about that?"

She places her spoon on the table and sits up staring at me. Looks me right in the eye, she does.

"When did you become a *Business Associate*?" she asks me. Her voice has a sting to it, like Clorox bleach fumes in my eyes. She almost gags when she says 'business associate.'

"We got money. You complaining, poor little rich girl? You don't like this dump we live in? Homemade sewing is embarrassing."

"I'm sorry, Mom. I didn't mean...

I won't mention it again. I win the gold medal at the Regionals and the newspaper reporter who covers the competition is very complimentary. She writes about my grace and poise, costume, and smile. She writes that I remind her of another skater of promise several years ago who was destined for the Olympics. She says I move like her, attack my program like she used to do, even look a little like her, too. She'd also been well known for her beautiful costumes. She vanished from the sport scene. The reporter says she died in a plane crash in 1961 with the U. S. National Figure Skating team. I wonder who she was.

I compete in a couple more competitions and win before beginning my training for the Nationals. Coach Casey suggests I come to summer training camp in a few weeks. Then when school starts go "next door" to Colorado Springs for training school; I'll talk to Mom, I promise. My stomach is in a knot even thinking about how this is going to go. I catch her on a sober day, and I make Campbell's Tomato Soup for our supper.

"Mom, Coach Kathy and my trainer, Bob Lee, think I have a good shot at a National title. Well, that's a pretty big deal, see. Anyway, there's this summer training camp at the center and I could go there for a while this summer. Then when school starts they think I should go to Colorado. He said I could qualify for some financial help. Well, because it's probably pretty expensive, you know. So, I was wondering if—"

"Broadmoor is a good choice for National training," she says, totally sober. "They have a good summer program, too. You should go there."

I stare at her. How does she know it's Broadmoor? I hadn't said that. She doesn't ask how expensive it would be, or even where it was. I guess she can't wait to get rid of me.

Chapter Thirty-Three

MARIAN

What will I do without Sienna here? I've got to sober up. I need to do something. I'm going to make her some more costumes. She must be good, going to the Nationals. I thought she'd give it up long before this. Most girls give it up before this. It's really a lot of hard work. She'll be gone a month. Maybe I can get myself shaped up by then. Do something to make her proud of me. I'll quit drinking. I could if I wanted. Yeah. I will.

I hate it when I'm rude or snotty to her. None of this is her fault. She's really a sweet kid who deserves better than this. It's just unfair that's all. We might be skating together – or I'd be skating with Michael – if this leg— *Stop it! That's someone else's life. Leave it alone, Marian.*

No drinking today. Uncle G said moderation; don't let the opponent have the edge because you're hung over. I never empty my glass. I always keep my drinking under control. Sienna walks around picking up glasses all the time. None of them are completely empty. I hope she notices that.

No pills today. They make me groggy and sleepy. One time when I was groggy, I ran the sewing machine needle through my fingernail. But I need the pills to control the pain. I've got a month. I'll do it. Of course, if a headache comes on, then I'll have to take my medicine.

Sienna hates that I keep the draperies drawn. She doesn't like it dark in here. I tell her it helps my migraines. I don't tell her that it also keeps people from looking in. She'd want to know what people. I've thought about getting us a Doberman. But this house is too small. I think about keeping a gun; but I don't ever want to see another one. I know they're out there, trying to find me.

She thinks I don't want to see her skate. Mama never wanted to see me skate, either. Mama never went anywhere. Neither do I. *Am I turning into Mama?* I'd love to see Sienna skate, but it would kill me to be there and not be on the ice. I just couldn't do it. I've never been a spectator. And why would I want to embarrass her with an ugly crippled mother? Kids would stare and say, "*That's* your mother, Sienna? She's pathetic."

I get out the phone book, a notepad, and make a plan. Finally, my own plan. One I came up with on my own. I make the call. I'm taking charge of my life. I take a shower, and shampoo my hair, and even put on a little lipstick. There's a knock on the door. I take a deep breath and answer it.

"How do you do, Mrs. Starr. I'm Ryan Anderson, manager at Lakewood Club. Thank you for calling me."

Mr. Anderson, the ice rink manager, steps inside. How

many years have we lived here? He might be the first guest I've ever invited in. I'm dressed in decent clothes this morning and discover I've put on some weight. I wear a long skirt to cover the ugly leg brace. I don't want him feeling sorry for me. I don't really have anything to serve with the coffee, but we sit at the clean table and I show him my sketches and samples.

He spends two hours here, and when he leaves I have a contract and a job. My signature hops around like squiggles on the ice made by a dull skate blade. I hope he doesn't notice. I need a drink to celebrate, then I'll get started ordering materials. The month goes by quickly. Soon Sienna will be on her way home.

Deanna Klingel

Chapter Thirty-Four

SIENNA

Camp is cool – a lot of fun. I try not to think too much about Mom at home. I really need all my concentration and energy to focus on all I'm learning. And Mom was right, I get automatic fall enrollment after summer camp. How on earth did she know that?

My first time in the lunch line, the elderly cafeteria lady is scooping me up some macaroni and cheese and stops with her spoon mid-air.

"Well, lookit here," she says. Her name tag says Freda Rose; she's looking right at me. "Well, honey if you don't make time stand still. Rosalie, git over here a sec and have a look."

Another cafeteria lady is pulling her hair net on and she comes over and says, "Whatchuwant?" to Freda Rose who nods in my direction and Rosalie looks at me a minute while I'm waiting for my macaroni and cheese.

"Well, whatchu know 'bout that. Girl, whatcher name?"

I tell her. They both laugh like they think that's a funny name.

"Well now, Sienna Starr, you gon' be a real star, mark my word 'bout that. You're the spit and shine of another little star, an Eyetalian, who used to come through this line, long time ago. She was the next great one, then she disappears right off the planet – 'long with all the others on that plane. Law 'ave mercy. So awful, that time was. Law' a' mercy, girl, you could be her. Look at that hair. We loves ya girl!" She plops the macaroni dead center in the middle of my plate, laughs some more and passes the plate on down. Every time I go through the line she's all howdy do and how are you, and extra portions of everything. She's like my personal cafeteria friend. I go in to say good- bye to them both before I leave camp. They actually hug me and say, "till next time. And there will be a next time." They *hugged* me.

"Hi, Mom! Did you miss me?"

"Of course I did. Did you have fun?"

"It was the best. I learned so much, I can hardly believe it. My figures are so much better now. Wait 'til you see ... well, I mean ... they're better. I made some new friends, too. I hardly stuttered at all. The summer camp guest speaker was David Jenkins who won gold at Squaw Valley. All us girls were swooning. He's the most famous person I ever met, and the handsomest guy I've ever seen. You should see him, Mom. He's like a movie star or something. He talked about never giving up on your dream to be a skater. I never will.

"Some of the coaches think I should go there to the training school. I can get automatic enrollment since I went to summer camp. They have regular school there, too. But I know, it's expensive. And I really like my rink here. I think only rich kids can go there."

"You can go there." Mom's face is expressionless.

"No, Mom, you don't understand. I'd be living there in Denver. I'd go to school there and train there, and it costs a lot of money."

"It's not in Denver. It's in Colorado Springs. If you want to go, you can go. I want you to go."

How'd she know it's in Colorado Springs? We have that kind of money? "Well, okay, I'll get the information about it and bring it home and then you can see what it's all about and see how much it costs." *I'm sure she'll forget by tomorrow that we had this conversation today.*

"You aren't the family accountant, Miss Smarty Pants. I know how much it costs, and I said you can go. I want you to go. I have money, Sienna; I'm not poor."

"We're not? I'm sorry, I mean, are you sure about this, Mom? I mean … I'd love to go, I just thought—"

"Well don't. That's *my* job. I'm in charge here. It's settled; you're going."

Mom's making me some new pajamas, some slacks, a cute vest to match, and I ordered some underwear and shirts from the Sears Catalog. Mom says 'pick out a purse.'

"Why do I need a purse?" I ask her.

"You're too old for a diaper bag, Sienna. It's time you had

a big girl bag. And that's called a purse. Time to grow up."
She's being really sarcastic. I hate when she does that. But I
order a purse from the catalog, to make her happy.

When I have everything lying on my bed to be packed, I
find a diary with a key lying on top of two beautiful new
costumes. The diary had the first few pages torn out.

"Thanks, Mom. I'll write, I promise."

"Just write when you can. Do good in school and
graduate, that's the first thing. Train as hard as you want to, for
the next thing. Decide things for yourself. And, Sienna ... have
fun. Life is uncertain. Don't be afraid, Sienna. Just look your
fear in the eye. Take charge. Don't ever let your fear show. Just
look it in the eye."

"Thank you, Mom. And, Mom? Take care of yourself.
Please?" *How will you manage without me? Look my fear in
the eye? Did she just make that up?*

I got into the taxi and I waved good-bye to Mom. I wish
she could go places with me, but her leg brace makes that too
hard. And, the other things do, too. It's best if she stays home.

Chapter Thirty-Five

I love my open sunny dorm room, the modern classrooms, and the lively dining hall at the Broadmoor Training Center. The student center has a piano and some of the students play and we sing along. It's the happiest place I've ever been.

It's also very competitive; the competition is really what it's all about, after all.

I try not to think about Mom, lying home on the sofa, snoring and drooling in the dark. I wish she could see how nice it is to have sunshine in the room and hear people singing. I wish she could see me skate. I wish she wanted to see me on the ice. I've even learned how to take care of my new boots. A skate technician they call Ziggy gave a little seminar about equipment.

They call him that because of the sharp edges and points he hones on the toe picks and edges to help us zigzag better. I've heard he's the best skate tech anywhere. Ziggy fits my boots, teaches me to wax and oil, how to lace them tighter, shows me how he hones the blades and how to properly slide the wooden blade covers so the blades don't get dull. I enjoy learning the technical stuff. Ziggy's a lot older than me, he's a grown-up friend. When he takes his breaks, he sits with skaters who are off the ice, or between classes. Everybody likes Ziggy.

He's so easy to talk to. All the kids like to be with him. He talks about a lot of things. He's some kind of a counselor. He goes to a lot of churches and meetings with some of the kids. He's helping me with confidence and my stuttering.

"Mind if I join you?" Ziggy's handing me a V-8 Juice. I mark my page and close the book. He asks me about my home, my family, my training. It's so easy to talk to him, and he always listens.

"I live near Tacoma with my mom. My dad died at sea before I was born." Then something inside me starts to shake. It's a huge vibration, like an earthquake, and the tears are erupting. I bury my face in embarrassment and apologize. "I'm s-so sorry. I really don't understand what brought that on. I guess I'm homesick, missing Mom. I worry about her. I'm sorry, I apologize. I didn't realize how much I'm missing home; how much I worry about her."

"Tell me more about your mom," he says gently. He asks me a few questions, that don't seem real important, but he's interested.

"I'm so glad to be here away from her. But I feel awful that I've gone away and left her; she needs me, but I don't want to be around her anymore. But I miss her, and I worry about her. She doesn't take very good care of herself. She needs me, But she makes me so tired. Everything I say is wrong. I'm always starting fights. I don't mean to, it just turns out that way. I'll never be good enough to make her happy. I bring on her headaches. I think I *am* her headache." I sob and all the secrets run down my face with the tears. I tell him she sews … when she can.

"You mean, when she's sober?"

I stare at him. *Why did he say that? How could he know that? I never told anyone.*

"It's okay, Sienna. It's nothing for you to be ashamed of. It's your mom's illness." I stare while the tears stream down my cheeks.

"No one knows that about us. Nobody knows about our problems. How do you know?"

"I recognize the signs. I can help you, Sienna. Will you trust me to do that?"

I stare. *Why does he need to help me? I don't need help. Mom needs help. Yet, I always did consider it to be our problem.* I press my face in my hands.

"I understand." That's all Ziggy says. "I understand." He sits there beside me while I blow my nose and pretend to be studying, like nothing I said really mattered that much to me.

"May I pray for you?" he asks. I nod. He touches my arm with his hand and prays. Maybe God listens to Ziggy. I haven't been on speaking terms with God for a while.

"What time are your classes over this afternoon?"

"I'm finished at three, and then I have ice time at four thirty."

"I'll pick you up at six o'clock in front of your dorm.

Casual clothes." He strolls off.

"I understand." That's what he said. The words coat my stomach, like Pepto-Bismol. At six o'clock I'm on the front steps and Ziggy's there on a bike.

"Hop on."

I sit side saddle on the flat book rack over the rear tire of his Schwinn Phantom. He pedals to the edge of the campus, then turns the corner onto a neighborhood sidewalk. On the corner of the next block sits an odd little building. I can't decide if it's a church, a house, or a coffee shop. It turns out to be all three.

Inside, Ziggy introduces me to several people, Steve, Judy, Edith, Bob. Some are my age, some are his; most are somewhere between. We seem to have nothing in common, none are skaters, some are students, and I wonder what kind of gathering this is. Some church perhaps, or friends who get together regularly for coffee? It's a strange evening for me. The meeting opens with a prayer. Then someone presents a short program about being powerless over alcohol and lives being unmanageable. It's interesting. A smiling girl named Judy brings me a lemonade. For the first time ever in my life, I'm telling someone what my life with Mom is like. Judy is my "sponsor." We talk almost every day the next week for a few minutes.

It turns out that what everyone here has in common is mom. All these people have lived with someone like my mom.

Many of their stories are much worse than mine. Some aren't as bad. But our commonality is that even though we don't swallow the pills or the alcohol, someone important to us does, and our lives are affected. We all need someone to say, "I understand," and "it's not your fault." We all need that Pepto-Bismol feeling. Ziggy picks me up regularly to attend these Al-Anon meetings. I'm astonished that these strangers are willing to tell about themselves and their families. And I'm even more astonished that I want to tell them about me and mom. And they even pray for my mom. I tell Ziggy and Judy how I skate with a passion, with speed, with daring. It's those moments of intense concentration on the ice that Mom can't spoil for me. I skate with grace, rhythm, and flow. In those soothing moments I allow myself to love her and not fear her rejection. On the ice I'm safe from her torment, and confident. At home, I'm always her disappointment, her headache. I stammer and worry that I'll say the wrong thing, apologizing when I do. They understand. I feel a huge burden lift off me.

Al-Anon meetings turn my topsy-turvy life around so that it begins to make some sense. I stop wondering what I do to make Mom angry and realize that I don't start the fights. I quit apologizing about her migraine headaches that she has because I was born. Migraines, and hangovers, are not my fault. I learn it's okay to feel cheated that I've never had a friend come to my house. I learn to forgive her for all the hurtful things she says to me when she drinks. I tell it aloud to someone who understands that I hated her when she passed out on the sofa, drooling, while I stood on a chair and made myself Cream of Wheat for supper or how I used to talk to her empty chair, telling the chair about my school projects. I can say to these strangers how unfair it is that the child took care of the adult. They all know and understand because it's their story, too. *How can I ever thank Ziggy for this? How did he know? How did he guess?*

After a few weeks of Al-Anon, I make it a point to arrange my ice time so I can attend church on Sunday mornings. Mom used to send me to catechism class when I was young, but I've not been to Mass in ages. I'm surprised to see Ziggy there. Sometimes we sit with Judy and some of the others. Imagine that, I'm praying with friends. It's comfortable. It warms me. Life off the ice is becoming bearable.

Each Academic School class is preparing their presentation for the annual training center show. The dress rehearsal is scheduled just before finals and holiday break. We're planning an ice review of *Fantasia,* using Leopold Stokowski's music recorded by the Philadelphia Orchestra. I'm probably one of the only ones in the whole school who never saw *Fantasia* in the movie theatre. The music is so pretty, I can just imagine it. We all need flower-like costumes, but the catalog selection is puny. I recklessly volunteer Mom.

I write her a letter begging her, encouraging her to do it, and send her everyone's measurements and coloring, and ask for the cost, as if it's a done deal. *What am I thinking?* Daffodils, I write; my class needs to be daffodils. I hope the letter arrives when she's in a good mood and sober. But I know, sober doesn't necessarily mean a good mood, any more than a good mood means sober. And of course, there's headaches and the pain pills. She sends the sketches and costs and everyone is thrilled. I'm mostly relieved. But now I have nightmares of her letting everyone down. Mom isn't exactly dependable. The class will hate me. The week before the show I worry there won't be any costumes.

I'm planning to go home for Thanksgiving, like everyone else. I'm looking forward to it, I say aloud, but I'm really dreading it. When I'm away from Mom, I send her letters telling her about me and my life. I don't have to hear her response or her non-response. I just write it. When I'm away I convince myself that she's fine, that I'm fine, and that everything is somehow better. But once I get home, the truth has to be faced. And holidays at our house are never much fun. The Al-Anon group understands and bolsters my courage. It's the one place I can be truthful about my feelings.

I'm surprised to see Mom looking so good. When I comment on how well she looks, she acts surprised, shrugs, and says, "Well, I live alone now. Life's easier." There it is. Her hard life is my fault again. I spend most of the holiday at the skating rink and plan to leave right after Thanksgiving Day dinner, which I figure I'll prepare myself. I hope there's something to cook besides eggs, Cream of Wheat, and tomato soup.

Mom seems more sober than I remember. She's busy working on the order for our *Fantasia* costumes which she wants to have ready to send back with me. I'd like to enjoy her company, but her words hurt me deeply. I know I'll never forget them. I want to cry, but the only place I cry is with Judy and Ziggy. I can wait.

Everyone is thrilled with the costumes. I'm so relieved I nearly faint when the boxes are opened. Even though we look like a troupe, like we all belong together, no two costumes are exactly alike, just like real flowers. They all fit except for Molly who lied about her measurements. I put on my costume, and discover a label sewn into the seam. It's a fancy G, embroidered in gold on a black silk label. *How did Mom come up with that? Does it represent a gold medal? Is it special, just for me?* A tiny package wrapped in tissue paper is rolled up inside my costume.

'Wear it for good luck,' the little note says. The note is written on a cash register receipt for cigarettes purchased at the liquor store. The little necklace is pretty, very sparkly. I don't know anything about jewelry, but this is most likely from Woolworth's Five and Dime. But it is unusual; it reminds me of one of the old-time compulsory figures skaters used to do in competition a few years back. Mom, of course, wouldn't know that. I'll wear it for fun. I like it; it's pretty, and it's unusual for Mom to give me anything.

The afternoon of our dress rehearsal, I almost forget to wear the necklace. It looks good with my costume and just reaches the neckline. The stands are packed, as dress rehearsal tickets are available to locals at cheap prices and to the press for free. The music resounds in the arena and gives me chills.

The lighting technicians play with different color combinations and the whole thing gives me goose bumps. I'm thrilled and unnerved at being part of such a big show. Our entire class glides in a straight line, side by side, across the entire width of the ice and we travel the length of the ice doing precision footwork, like a junior Holiday on Ice. We're a long row of fresh and cheerful daffodils swaying and bobbing in the yellow spotlights. Tiny reflections off a huge hanging ball make pretend raindrops falling all over the ice. It's beautiful.

The Broadmoor's annual show is so well known in skating circles that famous skaters come to watch for enjoyment and to check out future competitors. Janet Lynn and Dorothy Hamill arrived this morning and all the girls are now planning to have their hair cut like theirs. They graciously signed autographs most of the morning. There's going to be a press conference right here at the center. Tom Wood who won Gold in 1970 is coming, and eighteen-year-old Scott Hamilton is arriving in time for the show. We teenage girls can hardly stand the excitement. Scotty really is cute. I'd be too embarrassed to talk to him, though.

For my solo part I have a long layback spin. I've been practicing since last summer. The pale yellow petals of my skirt lift into a circle, while the filmy underlay of pale green leaves cling to my thighs. I'm a daffodil spinning in the breeze. I don't know how mom knew how to make it, but it works perfectly.

Our class's costumes are the biggest hit of the show. Everyone's skating well and the audience loves us, stamping and hooting, standing up and whistling. We grin ear to ear. I'm so free on the ice. When the music plays, I glide into another world, where life is smooth and clean and there are no cracks in it, no debris to fall over. And I can forget about Mom.

We glide off the ice. Three reporters surround me, waving their notepads in my face. "How long have you been skating? Where do you live? How long have you been training for the elegant layback? What are your chances at the Nationals? Who are your parents?" I'm overwhelmed. While I'm trying to catch my breath, Ziggy appears, puts his arm around me and walks me toward the locker room. Two skaters watch us, glaring. One whispers in the other's ear. They laugh. I know they're laughing at me.

"You'll get used to that eventually," he says. "But it can be overwhelming."

The article in the local paper praises the entire show and mentions the youngest class, dressed as little red and orange poppies, all but disappeared under the red lights and technicians need to correct that before the real show. They say the daffodils in the rain were breathtaking. The solo performance of the daffodil class was outstanding, the reporter says, and the skater, Miss Sienna Starr, is a star to watch. The costuming for everyone was the best ever. I cut it out to take it to Mom. The article says to get tickets early, it's sure to be a sellout. I wish Mom could see us, and see how perfect her costumes are. I hope she'll be proud and maybe, just maybe ... would she be happy?

Another article about figure skating in general wonders what became of the wonderful star of the late 50's-early 60's. Gina Mangalli, a rising star, destined for Olympic fame. This reporter said she'd seen Mangalli in person in Chicago years ago and that Sienna Starr reminds her in many ways of that former star. Mangalli died in the airplane crash with the rest of the National team in '61.

"Their grace and poise, their speed and their joy on the ice is similar." Is this the skater that was mentioned in the other article? I wonder. Gina Mangalli? I've never heard of her. I guess she crashed before she got famous.

One of my classmates brings me an extra newspaper. "I thought you might want one to show your mom."

"Thanks," I wave. "What a thoughtful thing to do." Show it to Mom? Maybe. Probably not. I doubt she'd be interested.

I pull on my sweat pants and gather my things to head

back to the dorm, stopping at the public restroom first. No one is there, so I drop my bag on the floor and step into the stall. I hear someone come in, and from under the door I see four feet, then I watch my bag disappear. I hurry from the stall in a panic, yanking up my sweats. *My skates. My costumes. My class notes. My diary.* I dash around the bend heading for the door hoping to catch them.

"Wait! Those are my things." Hot pain shot through my knees; my legs buckled. My head yanked back, my hair is pulling backwards. I glance in the mirror. *Am I seeing double?* No. There's two of us wearing identical training warm ups with the center's logo on the front. One of us is also wearing a black plastic half mask from the Mardi Gras production months ago. I sit on the floor and looking up, I saw a third person, also in a warm up suit, leaning all her weight against the door.

"Wh-what are y-you d-d-doing?" I managed to breathe.

"Just want to talk to you," the first girl whispers. "We're a little tired of you. Beautiful this, perfect that. Future Olympian, my foot. We know who you really are."

"You're a fraud. Just a poor snot from the sticks, too shy to even talk to reporters. Can't even t-t-talk. Who foots your bills, sweetie? Who do they pay?" the one by the door spat hatefully. *What did I do to make her hate me?*

"I'm s-sorry. I d-don't understand what you are d-doing. I'm sorry."

"We want equality, that's all. Tell us who pays your way.

Tell us who your contact is in the press? Who's paying off the judges? Which ones are on the take? Just information. That's all we want. Level the field, you might say. Equality. Now."

"I d-don't know what you're t-t-talking about."

"Come on, Starr. You're not *that* good. You're part of the big payoff. We want in. Let us in and we won't hurt you. Keep us out and, well, maybe we'll keep you out, too. Fair's fair."

"Hurry up, someone's coming," the girl by the door hissed. She braced the door firmly. Someone tried to pull it, gave up, and went away.

My tongue freezes. My heart hammers. *What are they talking about? Keep me out of the competition?* I tremble. They could get me thrown out of the Federation.

"Wh-why are you asking me about payoffs? I don't know anything about that. And I don't know anyone who does." *I'm not a snot and I'm not from the sticks.*

"Ha. Nobody gets the kind of press you do. Not without backing. Not without payoff."

"This is a joke, right?" *You will not take me out. You will not destroy me.*

The two girls glare at me. They know me. *I must know them.* They look surprised that I answer back to them. *They think I can't, or won't, stick up for myself.* I can play this game, too.

"So you're jealous of me?" I ask, hoping I sound tougher than I feel.

"Jealous, of *you*? J-j-j-jealous? Oh, oh, I'm s-s-s-so-sorry!" she said with a sarcastic baby voice. "Don't insult us, Starr, just tell us who can be bought."

They think I'll apologize to them. What was it Mom said, *'look the dog in the eye? Don't let your fear show?'* Yeah. I stare them in the eye. Surprise, surprise, girls. Here's a new Sienna. I'm not stuttering and I'm not apologizing. I shove her away from me and stand up. I look down my nose at her. My knees throb, but I stand as tall as I can. I'll beat them at their own game.

"Maybe I earned it," I say boldly. "Maybe I work harder than anyone else. Maybe I *am* that good. Have you seen my triple? We've met, haven't we?"

The two girls look at each other, confused about what to do next.

"Do we know each other?" I ask again. "Oh, yes, now I remember you. Aren't those masks a little warm? Why don't you take them off? Are you hiding? You know what you're doing will get you thrown out, don't you? Are you afraid of me?" I ramble on, knowing it's throwing them off their game.

"Afraid of *you*? Hardly. Y-y-y-ou? S-s-s-ienna S-s-starr?" They both pretend to laugh, but they're nervous. My face burns, but I continue to look them in the eye. *You will not bully me. You will not win.*

"How much do you pay them, Sienna?"

"And *who* is on the take."

"I have no idea. I'm not involved in anything like that. You don't want to be either."

They step toward me. The door jerks a bit. Someone is trying to open it. I scream. The loudest scream I ever screamed. The loudest scream I ever heard.

The two girls smother me on the floor. One slams my head against the floor. Stars flash.

The door shoves open and a mob of skaters, spectators, police, and security guards all charge through.

"What's going on here?" I hear a dozen different voices say.

"Who screamed?"

"Is everything alright in here?"

"This girl here is making payoffs. Bribes the press and the judges. We caught her red-handed. She got scared and tried to run out. She must have slipped. Must have hit her head."

"Okay. Everyone out. We'll take it from here. Thanks girls."

The two girls brush themselves off, smile at the police, and head for the door.

"No, you don't!" I fly at them, knock one into the other and land on top of them. The policeman pulls on me, but I hold on tight.

"They are lying," I shout. "They attacked me. They have masks in their jackets. They're looking for a payoff contact. It's not me. They threatened to hurt me."

The security guards and police pull all of us to our feet, and give us a shaking.

"Yeah, yeah. Spoiled kids."

A black plastic mask flutters to the floor. The room is suddenly quiet. All eyes focus on the mask.

In the course of everyday news, this is pretty ordinary stuff, I suppose. But for me, this event is major news worthy. It changes a lot of things for me. I look in the mirror. I'm Wonder Woman. I just look the world in the eye. I never let my fear show. I don't apologize to the woman in the mirror. Never again.

Chapter Thirty-Six

I go to pick my boots up at the tech's counter. Ziggy says he's just going on break and asks if I'd like to join him. He pulls two root beers from the cooler and we slide into a booth.

"Nice column in the paper last week."

"I was very flattered by it, but also a bit embarrassed – and humbled."

"It was deserved; you were great. You're like a dream on the ice."

"Thanks, Ziggy. That's nice of you. I have so much to learn yet. For one thing, I need to learn some ice skating history. I've never heard of some of the old skaters they talk about in those columns."

"Well, they were before your time; don't worry about that. You just keep doing what you're doing; don't copy anyone else's style. Your style is your own."

I slurp the last drop of my root beer and wait for Ziggy to finish his. I finger my necklace absent-mindedly.

"Ziggy, did you ever have a girlfriend? When you were younger, I mean."

Ziggy looks up and cocks his head. "Now, why would you want to know about that?" He smiles at me.

"I don't know. I just wonder sometimes what it would be

like, having a boyfriend. I just wondered if you'd ever had a girlfriend."

Ziggy cocks his head in the other direction and squints a face at me.

"You did! I can see it on your face, you did, you did, didn't you? Tell me, Ziggy. How old were you? Did you kiss her? Did you skate together?" Ziggy gets up and clears our glasses.

"Ziggy, wait, please. I was just kidding. I'm sorry if I was prying. I was just teasing, really. Don't be angry. I'm sorry."

He smiles and shrugs. "I'm not angry. No need to apologize. You can tease and ask all you want. But the truth will never be told. Only the shadow knows." He makes a mysterious voice like The Shadow, on the radio, and we laugh. I know it sounds corny, but even though Ziggy is probably old enough to be my father, he's one of my best friends.

"Thank you so much, Ziggy, for being my friend. I'll always be grateful that you take me to Al-Anon. It's making a difference in my life. It's such a relief to not hate Mom. Hating can really be burdensome and tiring."

Ziggy smiled. "Yep. That's sure true. Remember, Sienna, you have the confessional available to you. Reconciliation can bring you a wonderful peace."

"I'm thinking about it, Ziggy. Thanks."

It's close to Christmas, cold and wintry, and the students are all studying for semester finals. I'm nervous about a couple of my classes, but I feel confident that I have a shot at honor roll this semester. I've not had coffee with Ziggy or anyone else in days, I'm so busy studying. Then in the middle of a blizzard I push open the rink doors, stamp my feet, and nearly run headlong into Ziggy, holding an armful of blades and boots.

"Hi!" I blow into my mittens and drop my books on an empty booth table. "Guess I'll have a hot cocoa before my ice time." The student behind the counter prepares my cocoa and I slip into the booth. As Ziggy approaches the booth, I pull off my hooded sweatshirt and my hand catches the chain of my necklace. The chain breaks, the charm flies into the air and clatters on the table, ringing the salt shaker like a tiny game of horseshoes. I grab the chain before it slides down my shirt. Ziggy rescues my charm. He holds it in his hand studying it while waiting for me to get situated. He holds it out to me, then stops, and looks at it again.

"Where'd you get this?" Ziggy is scowling.

"Mom gave it to me. It's just a cheap charm. She told me to wear it for good luck. So, I do, but I'm not really superstitious. It's not a big deal. I'll just put it on another chain or something. Here." He hands it to me and I put it in my pocket. I look up in time to see Ziggy, looking pale, turn, disappear behind the counter, and into the tech room, closing the door behind him. *What was that about?* I blow the froth to cool my cocoa, sip it, take my books and coat to the locker room, and dress for my ice time. Practice was so-so. I know I wasn't concentrating. Something about Ziggy's behavior is weird. I, of course, believe it must be my fault. It's my habit. That reminds me, tonight is Al-Anon.

Chapter Thirty-Seven

My friends at Al-Anon help me make a plan for my upcoming visit with Mom over Christmas. I'm surprised how many other people in the group have dreadful holiday memories, fears of making some more, and also need a plan. I've not shared my miseries of Christmas with anyone before. Who would believe that a child could be miserable over Christmas? Surely it has to be my own selfish doing. Aren't kids always happy at Christmas? But everyone here is making a plan to help them through another bad holiday. I'm not as unique as I thought. Somehow, it's helpful to know that. If they can do it, I can at least try.

At the rink the next day, Ziggy whizzes past me on the ice and gives me thumbs up "Good luck on your exams."

"Thanks, Ziggy."

Following my ice time, bundled in my hooded sweatshirt under my parka, and my books packed, I brace for the wind when I shove open the door. Ziggy's huddled against the wind just coming inside. I laugh at him. "What are you doing? You look like a robin that arrived too early in February – or a hobo." We both laugh.

"Coffee?"

"Sure." We go inside.

"Did you get your necklace fixed?"

"My what? Oh, that; no not yet."

"Maybe you should do that before you see your mom. She might ask you about it."

"Most likely she won't remember she gave it to me."

"When are you leaving?"

"My last final is on Thursday. I guess I'll get the six o'clock bus on Friday."

"It just happens that I'm going to Tacoma myself on that Friday."

"You're kidding! Are you going on the bus?"

"Actually, no, I'm driving."

"Oh, of course. You're an *adult*! I forgot it's just us poor students who have to take the bus." I'm teasing and being sarcastic, probably bordering on fresh and rude. "I'm sorry, Ziggy. I didn't mean anything—

"Want to catch a ride with me?"

"Really? Ziggy, that would be great. Are you sure? It's not any trouble? Why are you going to Tacoma?"

"Yes, I'm sure, and it's no trouble. I'd like the company, actually. I'm going to pick up an order of custom-made costumes. It's a new business out of Tacoma with a great new line. Management and the coaches are very excited about it. If the stock is true to the samples, we'll be doing future business with them. It'll be good that our teams will have something to choose from besides the General Merchandisers Catalog or

Columbia. They've been around forever and they get cheaper and drabber every year. A few days ago Sergio's tights split from the crotch to the knee." Ziggy smacks the table and busts out laughing. "That was so funny, Sienna, you should have been here. Old Sergio was storming and raving about cheap American products and how Italian products are superior—"

"Oh, right, I can hear that now, Sergio and his European superiority." We both laugh. Ziggy gets serious and changes the subject.

"Maybe I could meet your mom while I'm there."

"No! I mean, no, I don't think that would be a good idea. I mean, the holidays and all, she ... you know." I actually don't know what to say. Ziggy already knows about Mom, her drinking, her pills, and her unpredictable behavior. He already knows about my so-called home life with the curtains closed. Holiday cheer doesn't happen.

"Maybe," I say.

The next day I have a new cheap chain to put my lucky charm on. By the end of the day it turns my neck green.

"Like a leprechaun," Ziggy teases. "And everyone knows how lucky that is!" We laugh and I wear it home.

Chapter Thirty-Eight

We start our trip in good spirits and sing Christmas carols with the static on the car radio. Ziggy makes a couple jokes about my red shirt and green necklace. We snack on peanuts. I love how the landscape changes. The sky is dark and heavy and the radio warns of an impending blizzard.

"Maybe we'll be far enough away from here before it starts," Ziggy says. "Sure hope we don't get caught in it."

We stop at a roadhouse to get a bite to eat. There's no one here except the waitress and two truck drivers. They nod at us. One tips his hat to me.

"Lookin' bad out there," he says. "Better find you a place for the night."

"Hope we can stay ahead of it," Ziggy says.

"Nope. We're gonna get it. No getting away."

"What should we do, Ziggy?"

"I don't know really, Sienna. We need to get to Tacoma. It's a long drive anyway, but if we have to add another day or two ..." Ziggy groaned. "If the truckers are worried, we probably should be, too."

We gulped our burgers and went back to the car. Ziggy checked his map again.

"We've got plenty of gas since I just filled up a few miles back. I've got chains on the tires, but my car's not exactly a sled dog. Let's go as far as we can and when the storm hits, we'll just have to stop somewhere till it's safe to drive. Okay? Let's go." Ziggy hands me the brown paper sack with two pieces of pie inside with plastic forks. We'll eat pie later.

The late afternoon sky is dark and ominous. The wind is bitter. There are few vehicles on the road. The radio is playing tinny and scratchy Christmas carols. We try to sing along.

As we cross the border into Wyoming, the first snowflakes begin falling. The windshield wipers quickly clear them away. Ziggy puts on the headlights.

"This isn't too bad." I sing along with the Mitch Miller gang and conduct as Ziggy drives. When we get to Cheyenne, the snow nearly stops. Darkness is upon us. It doesn't look so scary anymore; looks like a regular winter night on campus. We're energized.

"We can keep going. This isn't bad at all."

We travel several more miles, maybe an hour or more. There are no lights, no buildings, no trees. I see nothing but darkness. Ziggy is concentrating on the road.

"Does anyone live in Wyoming?" I ask. I am serious. I glance over at Ziggy. Suddenly he lurches, makes a wide-open-mouth face, and slams on the brakes. We zigzag across the highway. Ziggy tries to straighten us out. In front of the headlights stands the biggest animal I ever saw. The car comes to a full stop, facing the direction we just came from. The animal leaps to the side of the road then stops to stare into the headlights.

"What is it, Ziggy? What is that?"

"Not sure. A deer? An elk? A moose? I don't know the difference. Do you?"

"I've never seen any of those things. It sure is pretty. And big. I'm glad we didn't hit it."

"If we had, I think we would have been on the losing end," Ziggy mumbles.

We sit there a few minutes more. The animal gets bored looking at us. It nibbles at some roadside plants sticking up through the slush, then it ambles away.

Ziggy turns the car around, and we head off through boring Wyoming.

"How much farther, Ziggy?"

"A long way."

The radio is off and I'm feeling sleepy surrounded by darkness. I don't want to abandon Ziggy, but I soon doze. My head knocks against the window. I don't know how long I snoozed, but now it's even blacker outside. I look ahead and see a heavy snowfall in front of the headlights. They look black instead of white. They seem to come straight toward us.

"We'll be stopping soon, Sienna. Keep an eye out for any kind of motor inn. We'll need one."

I'm watching, but there are no lights anywhere. The

weather is getting worse with every mile. We drive all night
through snow, fog, rain, sleet, depending on the elevation. The
trip is a nightmare. The tenseness in the car is like a rubber
band stretched to its limit. I think any minute the doors might
explode off their hinges from our stress. Ziggy can barely see.
He flips on the bright lights, the low beams, the fog lamps, and
then starts over again, doing anything he can for better vision.
The windshield wipers freeze in the sleet and we pull off the
road to yank them loose. We hardly speak for hours while I
chew my fingernails to the skin. Ziggy grips the wheel and
concentrates on the road. I feel dizzy from squinting through
the swirling, driving snowflakes. They are coming straight
toward us like a tunnel.

"Maybe we should just stop," I suggest.

"We'll be in bad trouble if we get stranded out here. Don't
you notice how desolate this is?"

Yes. I do notice that. Parts of the road are slick. The car
slips and slides. Ziggy drives down the center so we don't fall
off the cliffs. Some of the roads are so steep, we're sure the car
will slide backward going up or slide down the inclines. The
chains make a monotonous ringing noise. I imagine how steep
the drop offs are. I can't see them. Other parts are covered in
snow and we can't even see the edges of the road. In places the
snow has drifted as high as the car. Ziggy drives carefully
around the drifts staying in the bare spots that have blown
clean. It's treacherous. Ziggy's two hands squeeze the steering

wheel. I imagine he's perspiring. I know he's praying.

It's four o'clock in the morning when I think I see lights ahead. There are large signs appearing along the road but the snow covers the words. They look like white lollipops. We see blinking red lights ahead.

The Utah State Highway Patrol tells us we must turn off this highway. The road into Salt Lake City has been plowed, sort of, but the highway is now shut down. We drive into Salt Lake City. The city is nearly buried in heaps of plowed snow. The main road and parking space are clear.

"What will we do?"

"Sit tight, Sienna. I'll ask someone."

"Who's walking around in the snow at four thirty in the morning? There's no one to ask."

Ziggy looks around, shivers, and gets back in the car.

"We'll have to sleep in the car." Ziggy goes to the trunk, pulls out his picnic blanket and dashes back to the car, beating the snow from his shoes and socks. He spreads the blanket across the two of us, takes a deep sighing breath, and lays his head back against his seat.

I know it's light, even though the dark clouds are still spilling a light snow and the windshield is completely covered over with a gray blanket of snow. I'm hungry. The peanuts are gone. I try to wipe a peep hole in my window. I need to go to the bathroom. I try to open the door. It won't budge. I move the handle up and down and lean into the door. I bang against it with my shoulder. It's freezing in here. I blow into my hands and try to kick the door open.

"What are you doing?" Ziggy complains. "Go back to sleep."

"I can't get out, Ziggy. The door is iced shut."

"Really? I thought it was cold, but not that cold." Ziggy tries his door. It's iced shut.

"I have to go to the bathroom. I have to get out of here." I sound a little panicky. I'm scared.

Ziggy turns on the ignition. It hesitates, sputters, and gives in. He turns the heater on high. Every few minutes we try the doors. He tries the windshield wipers to clear away the snow. They don't move.

"What time is it anyway?" I ask.

"What difference does it make?"

"You're grumpy this morning."

He smiles. "Yeah. It's a rough morning." He tries his door again.

"What's that?" I hear pounding. Scraping. Thumping. The snow is being pushed and pounded off the windows, and a man is looking in at us. His red and black checkered hat with ear flaps, covers his entire head with sheep skin. His thick muffler covers the lower half of his face. His eyes and bushy brows study us. Somewhere from beneath the muffler a voice is breaking the silence.

"You folks okay? How can we help you?" Other faces are

appearing, eyes peer between hats and mufflers.

"Can you open the doors?" Ziggy asks.

Three on each side of the car, scrape the snow from the windows, and finally open our doors.

"Bad night out there, wasn't it."

"It was all that," Ziggy answers.

I look around the parking square at the closed businesses.

"You need anything, the city police station is right over there. They'll help you."

I dash to the police station, use their facilities, and join Ziggy for a cup of the police post coffee. When my cup is empty, I suddenly remember. I hate coffee.

By noon the town diner is open for business. Ziggy and I woof down a plate of the best eggs in the west. By early afternoon the gas station is open. We fill up the tank. By late afternoon the highway out of town heading northwest is clear and we're ready to move on.

"Be careful out there," the policeman warned.

"I wish the sun would come out," I wish aloud. "I don't like these dark clouds."

Ziggy doesn't answer. He's driving the speed limit and hoping for the best. Part way through Idaho, we get the worst.

The snow is heavy, hard, and constant. The highway is covered quickly, and the wipers do their best, but it isn't good enough. Ziggy hunches over the wheel, and tries to see through the sheets of snow. As the window beside me gets smaller and the road in front more dangerous, I feel claustrophobic, like an eskimo in a little round igloo. I need to help Ziggy. I pray. The mountains are so high, we must be almost to heaven. Maybe God is close. All through the day, through another state, and into the evening, the snow turns to sleet. Oregon.

"Are we almost there, Ziggy?"

"No."

"I just thought of something. Remember that sack with the pies in it? How many days ago was that? We forgot to eat the pie. They're still in the back seat on the floor. Let's eat them."

We are barely going ten miles an hour. It will take another day or more to get there at this speed. If only we could get a break in this weather. Every few miles we see cars off the road, abandoned or banged up. We pass a turn-off where travelers can view the scenery on another day when they can actually see. Ziggy pulls in. He puts on the brakes and the car skids into the curbing.

"Nice stop."

"Where's the pies?"

"Lovely picnic spot." I reach into the back and bring out the sack with the pies and plastic forks. "Cherry or apple?"

While we eat, a big piece of road equipment rumbles past throwing snow twelve feet into the air, and scraping the road almost clean. Behind the plow follows a salt truck spraying salt and gravel everywhere. Fine bits hit our car. It sounds the same as sleet.

"Let's go!" Ziggy said with loud enthusiasm. "We'll follow them."

"What if they aren't going our way?"

"This road only goes in one direction, Sienna honey, and it's going to Washington."

All of Ziggy's gloom and tension sail through the air with the plowed snow. We're driving on plowed, salted highway. The snow is starting up again. We follow the snow plow for hours, it seems. We pass car after car buried in snow, abandoned. We see herds of deer, or whatever they are, in fields that are covered in deep snow. The plow keeps going, and so do we.

When the morning dawns with clear skies in Washington our heads are throbbing and we realize how hungry we are. We stop at a diner and eat greasy eggs and bacon, and slop some runny jam on our burnt toast. Ziggy orders a coffee to go. We splash water on our faces, and head for Tacoma. The snow has stopped. Some of the roads are slick, some haven't been plowed. But in some places we can now drive the speed limit. The sun is coming out.

Deanna Klingel

Deanna Klingel

Chapter Thirty-Nine

With every mile the knot in my stomach pulls tighter. It always happens when I'm about to see Mom. It started on my way home from school in the fourth grade. I never knew what I would find or how I'd be greeted. It's no different now. In the fifth grade I got off the bus three blocks early and walked home so friends wouldn't know where I lived. That gave me an extra three blocks of stomach pain. I'm thinking of asking Ziggy to let me out several blocks early. I never got close to my classmates or had many friends because I was afraid they'd want to come to my house. And sure enough, here's my friend Ziggy, wanting to come to my house.

"Once in the seventh grade, I did have a sort of friend," I babble to Ziggy. "I'd forgotten about her. She was an American Indian who lived on the reservation near Tacoma and took the bus in to school. She was a pretty girl, but she didn't do very well in school. One time when we had tutor buddies, I was assigned to be her tutor. She told me she couldn't do her homework at home. I said, "Sure, you can." She looked at me and said, "You don't know." I got to know her better, and she told me things about her home that I couldn't really believe. I thought she was making it up, how her Dad laid around in his underwear and said crude things to her, and how her mom screamed and yelled and sometimes took her school books and threw them outside. How she had to fix food for her younger sisters. The only thing that I remember that seemed to make any sense was that Rainy said this is what they did when they drank. She often had big bruises on her arms and neck. She didn't finish the school year. I hope someone has helped her, Ziggy. I hope she got some friends. I know she and I both thought it was best if we didn't have friends; we didn't want anyone to know. But now … I've changed my mind. I should have invited her to my house to do homework. But I couldn't. I hope she understood."

As if reading my mind, Ziggy says, "I know you're uncomfortable with me going to your house. I'm an adult, and I've seen a lot of things. Your mother won't shock me. But if you'd prefer, I'll just unload your things and disappear before she sees me. I need to get to the costume factory anyway. But just so you know, I'd like to see your home and meet your mother. But that's totally up to you."

There are no nails left to chew, so I gnaw on my fingers. The knot inside pulls tighter. I think I might throw up before we get there. We pass the Tacoma city limit sign and Ziggy asks me for directions to Mom's house. But I don't know the way; I've never driven here, I was always on a bus or in a taxi. I'm really unsure how to drive to my home.

"Are you certain where we're going?"

"Actually, no. I'm not sure. There! There's the sign for

my rink, the Lakewood Winter Club. Go there. I can find my
way home from there."

Ziggy laughs and follows the signs. It turns out to be a
long drive. But once we're there, I can direct him via the bus
route, not necessarily the fastest route, but the only one I know.

"Down that road was my school," I point out. We drive
through a suburban neighborhood, pass a trailer park, and onto
a dirt road.

"This is the white trash neighborhood ... turn right," I
whisper. "I live here."

"Girl, you're about to dissolve. Take a deep breath. You
can do this. Remember Al-Anon. You're a different girl than
you used to be. One day at a time. You're going to be fine
today."

"But what if—

"No, Sienna, no what ifs. One day at a time, one crisis at a
time. Don't see trouble where there isn't any. You can do this."

"It's the little house set back from the road over there."
Ziggy slows and heads for my house. It looks so shabby from
the road. I'm glad there's snow because the grass was never
cut. There's a strip of masking tape across the front window.
She's thrown an ash tray or a bottle through it, again. I wasn't
here to go to the hardware store for new glass. *I should have
been here.* The garbage is tied up on the sagging porch. I
wasn't here to put it out to the curb. *I should have been here.*
Ziggy stops at the curb and says nothing, he just looks at me.

"You okay?" he says eventually.

"I need to go to the hardware store for a new pane of glass," I say lamely. The sidewalk hasn't been shoveled or salted. *Why would it? I wasn't here to do it. No one went in or out; what did it matter?*

"Ready? I'll unload your things."

I only brought one suitcase, my skate bag, and my book bag. I don't plan to stay too long. I stand there in deep snow on the sidewalk staring at the door.

"Would you like to come in, Ziggy?" We walk up to the porch and I ring the bell. The door opens and my mom stands there gaping. She obviously forgot I was coming. But she's dressed in clean clothes and her graying hair is combed and brushed into a French twist. She's even wearing shoes on both feet. She looks good, real good. Her stare fastens on Ziggy. I'm invisible.

"Mom? It's me, Sienna. This is a friend of mine from Colorado. Ziggy is the skate technician and he was kind enough to give me a lift. Ziggy, this is my mom, Marian Starr."

"I'm pleased to meet you, Mrs. Starr." Ziggy puts his hand out but Mom just stares at him.

"Mom?" *She seems sober; is she trying to be rude?*

"What? Yes, nice to meet you, Ziggy. Thanks, uh, thanks for bringing her. Nice of you." Mom's voice is husky from cigarettes and drinking. It makes her sound like the cackling Wicked Witch of the West. She sounds and looks much older than she really is. She's already turned away from Ziggy.

"Well, have a nice holiday, the two of you, and I'll see you in a week or so back on the ice, Sienna. Merry Christmas." He turns to leave and my mom, looking stunned, turns back and watches him leave. He unexpectedly turns back around.

"By the way, Mrs. Starr, I wonder if you can give me directions to my next stop. At least point me to the right side of Tacoma. The address is 55 Mulberry Lane. Any idea?

"Where are you going?"

"I'm going to a business. It's probably a mill or a textile factory. I need to pick up some skating costumes there."

"I see."

My mom looks pale and distracted. *Oh, I know where this is heading.* Her hands are shaking and her body is panic stricken. "Can't help you." She hurries inside and lets the door slam. She can't get into the house fast enough.

"Ziggy, I'm sorry. Mom doesn't drive and never goes anywhere. I'm sure she's just embarrassed that she doesn't know where it is or how to direct you. Ask at the gas station, they usually know. Thanks so much for bringing me. I'll see you in a couple of weeks. Thanks again. And, Merry Christmas."

"Sure. I understand." We wave. Behind me I hear a bottle crashing into the sink.

Chapter Forty

ZIGGY

I can sure see why the poor kid hates to go home. I saw the hands shaking, her mouth dried out. Did she even remember Sienna was coming today? I'll bet she was a pretty woman before she started bathing in alcohol. Sienna mentioned once that her dad had died in the war, so her mom has lived most of her adult life alone. Raising a child alone? Yeah, I'll bet that was tough. Probably not much money either; pretty poor neighborhood. The skating expenses must be tough to come by for her. Sienna must get financial aid of some sort.

I was pretty lucky that my mom and dad had each other and we had a stable household. I never did understand why my brother started drinking, though. *Where'd that come from?* He started drinking on weekends in college, and wham, he comes home an alcoholic. My mom blamed her parenting, my dad blamed the school. They blamed each other for not seeing it coming. They argued for the first time in their married life. The tension in our house was something brand new. Alan brought it in whenever he opened the door. He lost three jobs in six months, and Mom and Dad tried to help him and support him, gave him rent money, and he drank all the more, feeling sorry for himself. What a mess. How'd that happen? We didn't drink at home; I went in the army, didn't drink. Who knows why that happens? "God, have I thanked you today for AA and Al-Anon? That whole scene could have ruined our family without their help. Thank you, God. Thank you. And bless Mom, Dad and Alan today."

I wish there was a way Sienna could get her mom into a program. She could use a support team. She's crippled in some way. Wears a brace of some sort. Sienna hadn't mentioned that; must have been an accident or something. She looks about fifty something. It's hard to tell. Wonder if she ever had a job or did anything interesting. Must have been a boring life for her and Sienna. There's a Texaco sign. Let's see if they have a map or something.

"Whad'ju say it is? A costume place you say? Kinda late for Halloween."

I take out my invoice to show him the complete name and address. "It's called Gold G Creations. It's at 55 Mulberry Lane in Tacoma."

The attendant looked at the invoice. He pointed at the corner of the invoice where a fancy gold G was embossed. "S'pose the sign must look like this here … nope. Never seen it. You c'n look at the map if you want, but if I's you, I'd just call that there phone nummer and ask'm where they's at."

"Good idea." I hadn't noticed the phone number before. I hadn't noticed that logo imprinted before, either. I go out back and use his restroom, still studying the invoice. *I've seen that*

*logo before. Where? Where've I seen that? I'll walk next door
to the diner and get a coffee and a piece of pie. I need another
look at that logo on the invoice. It's familiar somehow. Where
have I seen that? It's going to drive me crazy, now, isn't it?*

"One dollar? Sure." I take out my wallet to pay for my
coffee and pie, pull out a five dollar bill, and wait for my
change. An old crinkled photo in my wallet stares back at me.
I've carried it all through my army years, to 'nam and back.
How many times have I tried to throw it away? That part of my
life is over forever and I don't need that old photo to remind
me of my wife – wife of the fastest wedding and shortest
marriage in history. We could probably be in the Guinness
Book of Records. Why can't I bring myself to throw this photo
out? I don't really want to forget her. She'd be in her thirty's
now. She had such beautiful hair. When I heard about the plane
crash, I thought my world had ended. I re-upped with Special
Forces 'til retirement. Carried this with me. Just can't throw it
away, I guess.

"Oh! That's—"

"Excuse me? Did you need something else?" The pie dish
teeters on the counter.

I stagger out the door, still staring at the open wallet. No,
It can't be. Gina, a teenager, standing in front of a huge iron
gate. In the center of the gate, a fancy gold G. *The* fancy gold
G. There it is. The hair begins to prickle on the back of my
neck. Where was this picture taken? My mind is racing too fast

to sort it out. No wonder that fancy G looks familiar. How many days and nights have I stared at this photo? I never even noticed … she looks like … Sienna.

"Wait!" I say aloud, and plop down in the front seat splashing my coffee. I look at the picture and try to calm down, but my hands are shaking. "What's going on here?" I take a deep breath and try to collect my brain, scattered in a hundred directions.

"Think. G … G … Uncle G. She called him that. That's it, Uncle G. What was his name? Giallo, Grillio, Garibaldi, what was that … Gina, Gena, Gera.Gino … Ginorelli? Giovanni. Giovanni. Big gold G for Giovanni … or something close to that. Was this where she lived? I never knew where this picture was taken. Michigan? The town where we got married? Let it go, Mike. It's just a coincidence." *A very big coincidence. Like the necklace?*

I drive off and look for a motor inn. I take a room, clean up, and stretch out. Tomorrow I'll call this number during business hours, pick up the costumes, and hit the road back to Colorado Springs and have Christmas with my family. Forget this; it's too weird. Alan's coming home with his family. I'm anxious to see them, especially my new nephew. Somewhere along the way, I might throw that old picture away. It's like carrying a ghost in my wallet. *But still …*

Chapter Forty-One

SIENNA

"Good morning, Mom. I made us some eggs and toast. Won't you sit down and eat them?"

"How'd you meet that guy you brought home. He's too old for you. You don't need a boyfriend."

"He's not my boyfriend, he's just a friend. A grown-up friend. He works at the Training Center. He's everyone's friend, not just mine. He only drove me because he was coming to Tacoma to pick up costumes. He says the samples look really great and everyone is excited about this new company. By the way, have you been doing any sewing lately? Everyone loved the costumes you made for our show. I brought you a news clipping that mentions how beautiful they were."

"Some. Some sewing. How long you staying?"

"How have you been, Mom?"

"You mean do I still drink?"

"I just wondered how you've been, that's all I meant."

"I've been working."

"That's great, Mom, what are you doing?"

"Sewing. How long have you known him? That guy. What's his name?"

"That's wonderful. I always knew you could be a success as a dress maker or designer. You're so good at it. I'm proud of you."

"What's his name, I said? That guy. Ziggy. What's his name?"

"I'm sorry, I don't know. He's just Ziggy. It's a funny story why he's called Ziggy. It's because he puts really fine picks ... those are the little zigzags on the tips of the bl—"

"I know what toe picks are. I'm not stupid."

"Oh ... okay, sorry, well, he does them so well, makes our blades so perfect they call him Ziggy because he helps us zigzag better. Isn't that a cute story?"

"Sure. How long have you known him?"

"Your eggs are getting cold. I guess I never asked him his real name. I should do that; he was in the army, I know that. He retired not too long ago. Why don't you eat and then go shower, Mom, and I'll clean up here. Then I'll shower."

"You think I need a shower?"

"I didn't mean that. I just thought ... never mind." The phone rings while I'm washing the breakfast dishes. I answer it, but it's the wrong number. He was looking for a business. After her shower, I ask Mom if there's anything else I can do for her, even though I know she'll be insulted that I think she needs help with anything, and then I go to the bathroom to shower. I think I hear the phone ring again. *Twice in one day? I can't remember it ever ringing at all.*

I hear her talking to someone. How odd. I can't remember ever hearing her talk to anyone in this house or on the phone. There was never anyone here but us, and no one ever called. I dress and come out as she's putting on her coat.

"You going out?" *Another big surprise.*

"Just a bit. It's business." I watch her drag her leg brace through the deep snow. I realize she doesn't use crutches anymore. Her limp is pronounced and she looks dangerous in the slush. *Where's she going?* She goes into the garage on the alley behind our house. I want to follow her, but I wasn't invited. We live separately, I need to remember that. I'm not responsible for what she does. I pull up every response, every little saying I can remember from Al-Anon. Mom seems sober this morning, but who knows what she'll be like an hour from now. Life is slippery here.

Before long Mom clomps back to the house, her metal brace covered in wet snow up to her knee, slush packed around the screws and hinges. The brace has a shiny black boot attached with screws. The boot has more lacing than my skate boots. *She must hate that.* I watch her wiping it off and I picture her lacing up shiny white boots. I wonder if she would've liked skating if she hadn't been crippled. Did she ever get to do anything fun before her leg got hurt? I wonder how old she was when she had to start wearing that ugly black boot? I wish she'd tell me about it. I know better than to ask. Once she said, "thank God you take polio shots." I wonder if she had polio. How many times have my questions caused a major blowup, followed by a drinking binge and a headache that was my fault? I don't ask. It isn't worth it.

"What are you staring at? Don't you like my fashionable shoe? Staring's rude."

I start to apologize, and then I let it go by. I'm learning not to take her bait.

"What would you like to do today? Anything?" She doesn't answer. I let it go. I decide to give the kitchen a good scrubbing. It will be sort of a Christmas present for Mom; one she can't throw away or toss under the bed. I'm wiping out the window sill over the sink when I see a car coming down the alley going very slow. I see it passing between the garages. I never saw it on the other side of our garage, so it must have stopped and parked directly behind it. The air is cold coming in the window, but I leave it up when I hear their voices. Two men are talking. It sounds like friendly chit chat, and the car doors are slamming. I hear the garage door spring shut and it's quiet. I'm putting the window back down when the garage door opens onto the alley again and I hear their parting remarks, trunk and car doors slamming. The car starts up and pulls away, crunching snow under the tires. I glimpse it in a flash of sunlight between the garages. We've never used the garage. Well, someone is using it for something. Mom must know about it since she was just out there this morning. *Could Mom be selling drugs in there? Mind – my – own – business.*

"Mom? Would you like to go see a movie today?"

"A movie?" She shrugs and lifts her eyebrows. She says nothing, but her look says, "Stupid idea. Why do I want to see a movie?" In the past I would have pursued it and felt hurt, but I let it go. If I want to go to the movie, I'll just go by myself. *And I think I will.*

I'm planning to announce my intent over lunch. But I answer the phone before lunch. *Three calls in one day?*

"Hello?"

"Sienna? This is Ziggy."

"Ziggy? How ... where did you find our number? Where are you? Is anything wrong?"

"No, nothing is wrong. Well, not exactly. Is your mom at home?"

"Of course. Why do you ask?"

"I need you to trust me, Sienna. Don't ask questions, okay?"

"Well, maybe. What's going on?"

"Did you bring your good luck charm?"

I laugh aloud. "Are you kidding? You're still thinking about that? I should just give the silly thing to you. You wear it and turn your neck green. I told you she'd forget it and I'm sure she has. Ziggy, I thought this was something important. Good luck charm; oh, brother. Now, where are you, anyway? I thought you were going home?"

"Never mind. I need you to do this for me. Put your good

luck charm under the door mat. Then leave. Give me an hour or so. Can you find somewhere to go?"

"Yes. As a matter of fact, I'm planning to go to a movie this afternoon. But the door mat? That thing is nasty. It's been laying there all my life. You'll never get the charm clean after that. What's this all about anyway? Are you making a practical joke or something?"

"I don't really know. Maybe nothing. Enjoy your movie. Oh, Sienna? I was just wondering: when's your birthday? Uh, huh. Year? No reason, just curious. Thanks, Sienna."

"Oh, I get it! Don't worry, I'm not going to see a forbidden film. You sound like a parent!"

Well, that's plenty strange. *What's he up to?* I put my necklace under the filthy doormat and the dust explodes when I drop it back down on the covered porch. I warned him it's nasty; he'll see. I'm sure it's not been swept since I left. I fix lunch for Mom and me, clean up, and tell her I'm going out for a while to see a movie.

"Good. I'm glad. I've got some sewing I need to get done." Just like always I'm keeping her from her work, imposing on her life. I want to talk to her about Al-Anon, and AA. It's helped a lot of other people. I'm such a chicken. *Just go to the movie.*

Chapter Forty-Two

GINA

I'm sure Sienna was hoping I'd go with her to the movie. Wouldn't you think that with all the money and social grace – or whatever it's called – that my family had, wouldn't you think we might have seen a movie? But until Michael ... Sienna thinks I grew up poor. Hmm. Maybe I did.

I've not had a drink in two days since she's been here. I've got to get some bookkeeping done this afternoon and start some sketches for a new order. Then ... then I'll reward myself with one drink. Just one. I can get it all done before she gets home. I don't need her harping at me about it.

Someone knocking? On the front door? Sam and Cletus are supposed to be packing up my next order and they use the back door. Who could be at the front door?

"Hello. Remember me?"

I feel the blood rising in my face and my hands tremble. "You're, you're Ziggy, Sienna's friend. Sienna's not here." I start to close the door.

"Well, perhaps you could invite me in."

"I'm not comfortable with inviting strangers into my house, and I don't know you. I have two factory workers out back so don't get any ideas. We have a gun in the factory." *If*

I'm rude enough, he'll leave. He has to leave.

"You really haven't changed as much as I thought, Gina. You're the same silly girl, who thinks I'm going to take advantage of you. That wasn't my style then, and it isn't now. May I come in?"

My insides are trembling and my outsides are melting. My voice is stuck in its box.

"I don't know what you're talking about. I think you should leave. Now."

"I think you do know, Gina. We need to talk."

"My name's Marian. What do you want?" The rasping noise is my voice trying to escape.

"Like before, I want to tell you four things. First, I want to tell you what a wonderful daughter you have. She's turning out a fine young lady, and you should be proud of her. Second, I want to tell you that I never forgot you, never stopped loving you. Third, I'd like to ask you for an explanation. And Fourth, I want to give you this – again."

There he stands in my broken down doorway, reliving the life I've sworn to never visit again.

"Ziggy … whoever you are, you have to leave. I want you to go, now. You *have* to leave."

"Why, Gina? Why? Tell me what happened." He walks through the door, pushes past me, and shuts the door behind him. He looks so much younger than me. I'm trembling. I'm out of control. "Get out! Get out now!" I scream. *I just need one drink. Get out!* I throw the ashtray in his direction and he catches it. A week's worth of butts and ashes spill to the floor.

"Gina—"

"You can't call me that. Don't ever say that name. It's not my name. Leave!" I shove past him to the kitchen. I open three cabinets before remembering where I last put it. I pour myself a drink, toss it down, and feel it calming me.

"That's not the answer, Gina." Why has he always been so damnably sane? I wilt. He takes the bottle from my hand and walks me back to the sofa. I sit next to him and stare into his eyes. But I no longer recall how it feels to not be afraid; I've been afraid too long. I stare into his eyes and I can't tell whose eyes are filling with tears, his or mine. Or maybe both.

"Gina—"

"No, Michael. You can't call me that. It's not who I am. Really. I can't be who you want me to be, who you think I am. I really am Marian Starr. That's how it is. It's how it has to be. Marian Starr, seamstress, a skater's *mother,* an old cripple, and an incurable drunk. I don't empty my glass though, so I'm not an alcoholic, not really. My uncle wouldn't like it. I just take it for the pain." I hear my babbling slur and the words are emptying themselves through my mouth without any effort or thought.

"I can't skate. Did you see my boot, Mr. Skate Tech? What about that?" I lift my skirt to display my brace all the way to my thigh. "Nice, huh? Not the girl you knew after all, see? Mistaken identity. I'm crippled, Ziggy. And my name's not Gina."

"What happened to you, Gina? What happened to us? Tell me about Sienna."

"None of your business. Your business is sharpening skates for winners. That isn't me. You need to leave and forget about this."

"Gina, please talk to me. I think Sienna might be my business."

"Didn't you hear me? I am not Gina. I'm no one. I can't skate! I can't do anything!" I scream and suddenly I wail. Crying. I have real tears, and I'm sobbing. I didn't think Marian could cry. She never has. But here she is, doubled over, wailing and carrying on like I don't know what. I can't stop.

I'm not sure exactly what's happening, and I'm not sure if I'm passed out or if I'm still trying to say something, but the noises are still coming out of me and the tears are pouring down. Michael's arm is around me. He doesn't say anything, he just holds me. He feels like my old friend. Vignettes of our past, mental pictures of better times, float past me. I want to grab them, hold them. But they're gone already. As the world begins to set itself right again, we're sitting on the sofa. Michael is holding my shaking hands and running his fingers over my chewed fingers and cuticles.

"You see how it is?" I say fiercely. I snatch my hands away from him. "You see? I'm a scary creature, and if you're smart you'll leave. Get your costumes and get out of here. Forget you've met Marian Starr. She's no good for you. Get out, Michael. Get out of Marian Starr's life. Get out!"

"Rest, Marian, just rest. I'll make some coffee."

The loud wail sounds like it's coming from a police bull horn outside. But it's me, wailing, flailing, "God help me!" I scream and collapse in a heap, land on my head on the floor, like a toddler in a tantrum. *Michael must have turned the lights out.*

Chapter Forty-Three

SIENNA

I really enjoy the movie and I promise myself to become a
movie fan. I eat Good 'N Plenty candy, popcorn, and don't
want it to be over. My new mantra: I love the movies. I'll tell
Mom I'm sorry she missed it and I hope she'll go sometime. I
won't discuss anything further. I wonder what Ziggy did
today? What on earth did he want that necklace charm for?
He's a real character. He's probably on his way back to
Colorado by now. I'm anxious to see those new costumes he's
picked up. Bet they aren't as great as Mom's, but I'm glad
we'll have something besides the catalogue specials to choose
from.

"Yoohoo, Mom, I'm back. You in the kitchen? Ziggy!
What on earth are you doing here? Where's Mom? I thought
you'd be gone already. Does Mom know you're here?"

"Here, have some coffee."

"I don't like coffee. Where's my mother?"

"She's in the hospital."

I always knew it was going to happen, sooner or later, it
was bound to. So why did my hand slap my mouth as if I was
shocked? Why am I too stunned to speak? I don't have to ask
why she's there. It's no surprise. But still … I cry for her.

"Ziggy, why are you here? What did you do? What did you do to my mom?" Ziggy doesn't answer me, but he motions for me to sit down while he sets the table for supper. He says there's no point in going to the hospital this evening, that she's "occupied with other things." He says we'll go tomorrow.

"You need to trust me, Sienna. I'll explain it all to you. But be patient, and trust me."

"Where's your car?"

"In the alley in front of the garage." He spoons his noodle soup.

"The garage." I blow on my soup to cool it down. "I'm going out there after supper. I want to know what she does out there."

Ziggy smiles. "I think you'll be quite surprised."

Surprised? I'm shocked. A factory? In the garage? It has heat and lights and sewing machines? When I saw it last it had a dirt floor and was full of junk and neighborhood cats eating the rats and pooping everywhere. My mother did this? *When was she sober long enough to do all this?* This is 55 Mulberry Lane? *I didn't know our alley even had a name.* This is the new Gold G Costume Design Company? My mother is a costume designer, and is running an actual business? *I can't believe it.* I pick up her advertising sheets spread out on a table. I look at her design boards. I see her orders thumb tacked to the wall above a sewing machine. A wooden crucifix is nailed to the wall above her orders. *Mom's?* The cutting tables have

measurements neatly printed along the edges. She has a big
recital order from the dance studio in town, and an order from
the Seattle Opera. More costumes for Lakewood.

One worker is oiling and cleaning a machine and the other
is wrapping finished costumes in tissue paper and placing them
in a box for delivery. My head is spinning. The label in my
costume – the big gold G – had come from this very spot. *So
everyone gets the big G sewn in their costume, not just me? It
doesn't mean gold medal? What does it mean? How'd she
come up with that design?*

"What are you thinking, Sienna?" Ziggy is sitting at
Mom's desk grinning.

I'm numb. When I say I don't know what to think, he just
says, "I understand. You're wondering how she did all this in a
drunken stupor. I think you're also wondering how she
managed to do it without your help, aren't you?"

I drop my head, feeling a bit embarrassed. Ziggy has a
way of sorting through my feelings quickly. He's kind of a
bottom-line person.

"I guess so. I mean, she's so mean and so ungrateful when
she's drunk it's hard to help her do anything. But when she's
not drunk, she's so disorganized and frustrated that she has
trouble getting much done before her next binge. If I'd been
here, I could've helped her do this."

"But she managed just fine without you." He looked up
and stared at the crucifix.

"Is she going to be all right? What will happen to her at the hospital? I hope they won't give her more pills. What happened, anyway?"

"Let's go back inside and let these fellows get their work done, shall we?"

"Why were you here? Was she sick? Did you see her collapse?"

Ziggy puts the tea kettle on Mom's greasy stove, rinses out a couple of stained cups, and we sit on the smelly sofa. Her factory smells fresh compared to this living room.

"I can't answer all those questions for you, Sienna. We'll go to the hospital tomorrow morning and talk to the doctor and see what's going on. Okay? Do you want me to stay the night, or pick you up in the morning?"

I look around the house. It's so quiet. Strangers are working in and around the garage. Mom is the adult. I'm the child. Most of my life that's been reversed. But now, I really want to be the child.

"Please stay."

Chapter Forty-Four

ZIGGY

Even with a fresh sheet thrown over the sofa, I can smell the alcohol and cigarette smoke. How many nights has Gina slept here, or tried to sleep here? How many times has she been sick on this sofa? How long has she been drinking? When did she change her name, and why? Does any of this have to do with me? Did she never want me to find her? How much does Sienna know? Oh, God, the wasted time … the wasted lives. I pray myself to sleep.

"Do you know the way to the hospital, Sienna?"

"I think so. Not sure, really. More coffee? Jam for your toast?"

"Let me clean up the kitchen. You go get ready. I'll look it up in the phone book."

We bump along in my old car.

"Isn't it funny how I've lived here all my life and don't know my way around? I never went anywhere in a car, and I've never driven here. Taxis and buses don't always take the most direct route, you know." She's chattering her way through her nervousness. She needs to do that; I let her.

"Have you lived here all your life?" *Be careful with your questions, old man.*

"Yes. I'm not sure when Mom moved here. Like I've told you at Al-Anon I don't know much about our family. Mom kind of goes off the edge when I ask, and so I've learned not to ask those questions. But she moved here before I was born. I was born in this same hospital."

"Did your grandparents or relatives ever visit you?"

"No. Mom's parents are deceased. I don't know about my father's parents, though. My dad's dead. I told you that before, right? He was a sailor and he died in a shipboard accident."

"Hmm hmm; you did mention that. Your mom's never told you anything about her life or growing up before you were born? How about your dad? Did she talk to you about him?"

"No. In fact, it's such a deep dark secret that when I was in sixth grade and our social studies class made family trees, Mom wouldn't even help me. I got a terrible grade because it didn't have anything written on the branches, even though I'd made the best tree. Kids teased me, saying I'd been hatched instead of born. I thought I might be adopted. But when I got older I realized that Mom would never have adopted a kid. She doesn't want one. Even when my feelings were so hurt and I was crying, Mom still wouldn't tell me any names to put on my tree. So I made up the names. I spelled them crazy ways that couldn't be pronounced and said they were immigrants from another country. I still got a bad grade!" Sienna's laughter has a familiar ring.

"I don't think you're adopted; you look a lot like your

mother."

"Can I tell you something really stupid? About my family, I mean? Remember those newspaper articles about me, the ones that said I reminded the skating world of another skater who'd disappeared? I pretended, in my head, that it was my aunt; that I looked like her, and skated like her. One of my friends at the center – you know Julie – has this really incredible aunt who calls her and writes her and sends her cookies and presents. She even made some little pink pom poms to put on Julie's skates. She shows up at competitions to surprise her. I'd love to have an aunt like that, so I pretend it's my aunt who was a famous skater who could've gone to the Olympics. Pretty stupid, huh?"

"Well, since you don't have any evidence to the contrary, I guess it could as well be true." I give her my reassuring adult smile. *Why doesn't Gina want her to know? Is it wrong for me to tell her what I know? And what, exactly, do I know? Nothing; absolutely nothing.*

The nurse at the desk wants to know if we're family. I would've told the truth, but Sienna answers quickly, "Yes." Nurse says to go in, but at eleven o'clock Doctor Silverstein will see us in the conference room. She points it out.

I say "Hello" to Marian, and Sienna gives her a cheerful, "Hi, Mom." She turns toward us and forces a little smile. She looks twice as old as me.

"Mom, I saw your factory. It's wonderful and I'm so

proud of you. Wow! Your own business. I mean it, Mom, I think it's great."

"How's the skating business?" She's looking at Sienna, and so far has managed to ignore me. Sienna looks shocked, as if she doesn't know what to say. I take it she isn't usually asked about the skating business. She tells her all about the show and her performances, her hopes and dreams.

Her mother says nothing, but she turns away and from my position at the foot of the bed I can see tears drop to the pillow as she listens to her daughter, perhaps for the first time in a long while, or maybe ever. She suddenly looks back to Sienna and smiles. It's a real smile. Sienna stops short in the middle of a sentence to take in its radiance.

"That's good, honey. I'm really proud of you. I really am, you know. I know how it feels to be on the winners' platform. I know how it feels to hold the trophy, and feel the cool satin ribbon around your neck. I also know how it feels to look into the stands and not see your mother there. I know how all that feels, and I really am very proud of you."

Sienna folds into the chair, mouth agape, trying to make sense out of all that while her eyes fill with tears.

Gina looks me directly in the eye. "C'mere, you, Ziggy, or whatever you call yourself. C'mere. Let me look at you. Mmm hmm. You look about thirty something. You ought to get more ice time, you'll get dumplings." Her laughter brings on a coughing seizure. We sit her up and help her breathe. Her IV pulses in a blue vein. Her hands look more like fifty than thirty-three. *I wonder how many people would be abusers if they could see how wasted they'd look at such a young age?* When her coughing stops and Sienna has successfully given her a drink of water, she tries to pick up the conversation once more. But I can see that the joy of the moment is more than she's ready for. The tears begin again.

"My first life wasn't bad enough. I had to be given a second life. That one's worse. I'd give anything to make it better. Is it too late for a third life?" She looks straight into my eyes. *There it is; she's asking for our help.* Her hands are shaking and perspiration drips down her neck.

I can see the confusion on Sienna's face. How I long to hold her and tell her about her mother, about me, her family. None of this is making any sense to her and it's all happening too fast. I squeeze her hand. For now, she needs to trust me. *Take this slow.*

A nurse comes in. "Excuse me, but Dr. Silverstein is in the conference room and would like to see you now. Mrs. Starr, how about a little rest?"

Sienna and I make our way down the worn hallway, past the linen closet and other patient rooms. It's an emotional walk, as I realize fifteen years ago my baby daughter took her first breath in one of these rooms. *I should have been here.* Dr. Silverstein looks like his name. His silver mane is distinguished and his handshake is strong. He's a head taller than me and his shoulders are square. I stand up taller and mentally agree with Gina that I need to work out.

I've heard this spiel about alcoholism and drug abuse dozens of times. Doctors must have to learn it by rote in residency. It's all very scientific and factual. The sick person doesn't believe it relates to him in any way. When he finishes, I introduce myself and explain that I'm the sponsor of many in Al-Anon, including Mrs. Starr's daughter, and I often present the AA and Al-Anon programs for school seminars and other community information meetings.

We talk for a long time and come up with a plan. Sienna squirms, and the doctor gives me a lot of leeway because my field experience tops his. I warn Sienna that this will be a tough go and not a pretty sight. We totally forget about Christmas and the costumes in my car. We're preparing to wage a battle side-by-side with Gina, Marian, Mom, my wife, whoever she wants to be, in this life, and in her third. Alone in the hall, I take Sienna's hand. "This will take lots of prayer, Sienna." We hold hands and I beg God to comfort and restore Sienna's mother. Sienna sobs softly.

The next day, Marian's very agitated, but she's moved to a different ward that's better equipped to deal with her drying out process. Sienna's a trooper. She cries a lot, but never when she's with her mom. There isn't a lot we can do for Gina right now, just be here, towel her off, and let her know it will be better. There is hope for her third life.

But Sienna? There's much more she needs. And it has to start with the truth.

Deanna Klingel

Chapter Forty-Five

GINA

Dr. Silverstein tells me I'm going to an AA meeting this afternoon on the fourth floor of the hospital. I'm nearly strangled with anger.

"Look," I tell him. "I've been cooperative and all smiley and cheery and sweet to everybody. I've been meaner than a snake and I know that, but see, now I'm not. See? I'm fixed. If I was an alcoholic, like you think, I'd still be mean and ugly, right? I wouldn't have fixed myself up like this. I don't need any meetings; I've got enough to do running my factory and sewing my costumes, and I really need to get back home and take care of business. I'm dried out and I'm going to be fine. I told Sienna to throw out any bottle she found at home. If she missed any, I'll throw them out when I get home. No meetings. I'm going home. I'm not an alcoholic. I've decided to stop drinking and I can do that by myself."

Sienna and Ziggy show up all ready to take me to the big deal meeting. They say they won't come to the hospital again until I agree to go. How many times have I said it … I am sick of other people making decisions for my life. I can decide this for myself. I go to keep the peace. There – okay, see? See that? I'm a changed person. This is going to be my first and last meeting. I glance over my shoulders every thirty seconds, certain to see a Gargoyle or a face from Fairfield's notebook. They're out there.

I attend the AA meeting on the fourth floor every day for the next few weeks. Ziggy and Sienna had to leave. I'm glad they were here, but I'm glad they're gone. Well, maybe. I miss them. I think I'm glad they're gone because there's still so much to be said, so much to be explained. If they aren't here, I don't have to face that ... yet. *How much has Michael told her? Is she going to hate me?*

After I go home, I return to the hospital every afternoon for AA meetings. I'm still not convinced I really need it, but it seems like some of my new friends in the meetings might need me to be there for them. *But why should I care about them?* I find out there's another meeting nearer my house in the old VFW hall every noon. Some of the others are thinking of going there also after our time is up at the hospital.

It's an odd sort of feeling to have friends, to be someone's friend. My friends are calling on the phone and I talk to my sponsor Sylvia every day. Until I set up my business, no one ever called on that phone. Sometimes I don't want it to ring. But after we hang up, I'm so grateful they called.

I get frustrated. I look in the mirror and wonder who that person is. I don't want to be her anymore. But who do I want to be? I don't want to talk to her. My past keeps burning a hole in my soul, trying to burrow deeper and deeper. If my new friends discover who I was in my other life, what then? Will anyone order costumes from a mafia princess? Who will want to pray with a crime family member? Burrow deeper, and don't get out. Ziggy says the answers aren't in a bottle, but it's the best place I know to hide secrets. Some days I get scared wondering where I'll hide the secrets now that the bottles are gone. I smoke, I pace, I shake. And for the first time in a long time, I want to talk to someone. I want to talk to the God of my childhood.

My business is going well. I have more orders than I can fill and I'm thinking of hiring a seamstress or two. I've ordered a new 1962 model of Singer sewing machine that does a lot of interesting stitching I've never done before. This could be a challenge, but now that I'm sober, I seem to learn new things faster. I may have to add a larger packing area out the back. We're getting too many boxes stored for pick up. There's a lot to running a business, but I was raised by a business man, after all. I'll hire some reservation kids to do the packing and labeling. I might find a couple of seamstresses on the reservation, too.

I put through a call to the FBI and ask to talk to Fairlane. He's retired they tell me, but they'll have him call me. *How dare he retire and leave me in this mess.* I'm not sure what I want from him. But somehow, I've got to get this all sorted out if I'm ever going to know who I am, and if Sienna will ever understand how my life turned out so badly. I really owe an explanation to Michael. But since I don't know how I want my third chance at life to turn out, I don't know what to say to him, or why I called Fairlane.

I'm relieved to have a letter from Sienna. She's back in school and working to get caught up. She writes that her teachers were very understanding about her mom being hospitalized over the holiday. She's preparing for the next competition. Ziggy caught thunder about missing work, but he's too good to be replaced, so all is forgiven and everything is smooth as ice in Colorado Springs. The ice is a little bumpy and cracked here in Tacoma.

Chapter Forty-Six

SIENNA

My coach and trainers aren't happy that I've missed so much ice time, and now I have twice as much to do in Academic School to get caught up. I'll do it, though, because the Nationals are coming up fast. I'm sure I can do this.

There are some new skaters on the ice that are all to-be-watched, according to the newspaper reporters. I've been interviewed a lot and my coach tells me to refrain from any speculation on how I will do, and to not offer any critique of any other skater. He and I are in agreement there. I'm practicing some very difficult toe loops and landing them consistently. I've selected my music and I'm working with the choreographer to design my program. It's got to be good. It's got to be the best.

I work like I've never worked before – faster, higher, wider, stronger, tighter. I pull my boots off next to the ice and walk barefoot to the locker room. My trainer sees me limping.

"Tight ham string?"

"No. Blistered toes."

"Thirty minutes."

"Yeah, okay." He's giving me thirty minutes to cool down, shower, and go to the training room for a massage. I'm too tired to care.

The massage is deep, painfully refreshing. When the trainer comes in he tells me to cut the ice time by half tomorrow. I start to object, but my exhaustion prevents the argument. I just nod in agreement. I dream my routine every night.

"All aboard for Vancouver."

We let out a huge cheer. There are twenty of us from Broadmoor on this chartered bus to the Internationals. Many of our friends aren't going, but since we've shared the ice for hours and months and years, they're all here to wave us off. I'm the reigning Junior U.S. Champion; this is a major deal. This will be my first qualifier for the next title.

"Good luck!"

"You're in our prayers."

"Safe trip."

"Bring it home, Sienna!"

I'm just moving onto the step into the bus when Ziggy appears. He hands me my little necklace charm.

"Wear this … for luck. Your mother would like that." And just like that, I'm on the bus and Ziggy's gone. The little charm is on a new gold chain, and it's polished. It glitters in my hand like real diamonds.

Our hotel's not very fancy, but no one complains. We won't be spending much time here anyway. We have a get-acquainted social this evening for a chance to meet all the competitors. Some are like old friends we've met and competed against and watched as their career advanced, or didn't. Others are newcomers, some already making headlines, others still unknown.

We are all giddy, nervous, trying to act cool and calm, like we have it all under control. But everyone knows it's the ice that's in control. The best program, the best skater, the best team, is just as nervous as a novice, and their moment of glory can end just as fast. Our lives are dedicated to contributing to the sport, and the fame, the glory, and the danger that goes with it.

By evening, we are all so tired hardly anyone stays in the lounge for the socials planned for all the teams. They give us nametags to wear and ask us to talk and mingle with everyone. Someone plays the grand piano and waiters pass plates of tea sandwiches. Mostly, everyone just wants to get to their rooms to go to bed.

I concentrate totally on skating and keep Mom out of my head. I have to. I can't skate with baggage. After three days, I'm exhausted, but so exhilarated I scarcely notice the exhaustion. I've eaten meals with the best skaters in the world. I'm totally inspired. My ordinals have been excellent, but I'm skating against a field unlike any before. Today has to be my best ever performance. I'm ready.

"Hey, Sienna, you see the paper this morning? Interesting

read." It's one of the skaters from the Midwest. Out of costume I don't recognize which one for sure, but she smiles and hands me a rag newspaper from Chicago.

"I didn't know tabloid papers had sports sections," I joked. Mostly it's gossip. I carry it into the locker room and lay it on the bench while I unload my gym bag. I glance at the front page. *Who is that?*

I slowly lower myself to the bench, staring at the photos. *"Whatever Happened to America's Sweetheart of the Ice?"* The page is laid out like a scrapbook with photos plastered over each other. Placed at an angle another picture shows a skater in a beautiful costume doing an elegant layback. Then a tilted more recent picture of the same skater doing the same thing. *No, wait, that's me.* Then the last is a picture of a small group of skaters having coffee at the Broadmoor. I'm with them. I don't get it. *No, that's not me. I don't have a shirt like that.* This is an old photo, you can tell by the hairstyles. But it could be me. *What is this all about?*

Remember what my trainer says about these kind of newspapers? Never take them seriously, he's warned all of us. "Keep your noses out of the Paparazzi crap," he always says. "They make it look like you're doing bad things when you aren't. They insinuate sin," he says. "The Paparazzi will destroy your concentration, as well as your reputation. Stay away from them. Ignore them," he told us all. But there I was, on the front page. This skater is me, and this is at the

Broadmoor. But who is this other skater? She looks like me, but it's not me. Why are these other photos in this same layout? Who are these bad guys in handcuffs? They look like mafia guys. What kind of a screwy page is this? Where's the article? Where do they get this trash? I have to throw this away and get my concentration back. *I cannot think about this now.*

My stomach is tumbling. Would I feel this way even if I hadn't seen the paper? Maybe it's just nerves after all. That skater did this on purpose. A friend wouldn't have shown that to me today. The rest of this day, which should be the most exciting day of my life, rolls past me like the movie theatre newsreel in black and white, in shades of gray, handcuffs, and ice skates.

I dress in a beautiful costume, custom made by Golden G Costume Design of Tacoma, Mom's own design, created just for me. It fits like my skin. My new boots wear custom-fitted, matching boot covers, Mom's own idea that everyone is copying now, in stunning colors to match the costumes. I swallow three Bayer aspirin for my headache and I pace. I talk to myself; I close my eyes and watch me perform my entire program. For the first time ever in my skating career, I really wish Mom was here. I keep getting flashes in my mind of the newspaper. *How is Mom managing her sobriety without me?*

The audience loves my performance. My three days are tallied while I wait. My coach joins me and puts her arm around me.

"It was good, Sienna, real good. Now we wait and see."
What we see is that most of the judges awarded just a little less
than we hoped. At the end of the day, Sienna Starr is a silver
medalist at the U.S. Nationals. I'm thrilled.

"Not shabby, not shabby at all," my coach proclaims.

Little by little, the earlier part of the day begins to creep
back into my consciousness. Mom; I'll call Mom tonight. I
pose for pictures, shove my flowers in my skate case, and pack
to go home.

There's no answer at Mom's house. I feel strangely
disappointed. But tonight, I really want to tell her … what?
What exactly do I want to tell her?

When the bus pulls into the parking lot in Colorado
Springs, it looks like most of the town is here. Well, at least the
skating fans. The next generation of hopefuls, the kids who
hang out at the Broadmoor Training Center, in awe of the
world famous coaches and skaters. We sign autographs, act like
a team, then disappear into the inner sanctum of the locker
room. Later, I'll call Mom. I look around for Ziggy. He isn't
here.

"Attention everyone," the manager bellows. "Everyone
has the next day off to rest and recoup. Tomorrow we'll be able
to see movies of our performances. This is a wonderful new
training tool; we can actually see the tiny mistakes that cost us
points. The trainers say these "videos" are going to be the best
training tool ever. Two o'clock sharp. Sleep in, eat well, and

we'll see you at two. Congratulations to all of us."

There's no answer on Mom's phone. *Who's minding the business?* She told me that she had put an extension phone into the garage. I still call it the garage, though it really is now a factory. I picture Mom passed out on a pile of costumes smelling like booze and cigarettes. *How could I have been so stupid to think this would last?*

The last few times I talked to Mom she seemed totally sober. She says she's been going to AA regularly and her friends and sponsors call her every day and pray with her. Lately she's been going out a little bit for dinner with her friends. No drinks, she says, just dinner. She's surprised that a cripple in a brace can enjoy friends and dinner. She even went to a movie to see *Jaws*. She says it's the scariest thing she ever saw. Worse than a hangover nightmare, she says. No drinks, just a movie. No one seems to mind her brace, she tells me again. "I can't imagine why they want a useless old cripple who hobbles along with an ugly brace for a friend," she says.

"Mom, I don't think they see you that way. They see you as a talented designer who is a nice person. Someone they like to have for a friend."

"Get off it, Sienna."

I've been really hopeful. Now, where is she? I still go to Al-anon just to stay with the program. I don't feel as overwhelmed by Mom and her drinking when I'm not around her. But Ziggy says I need to try to keep going; that I'll be stronger when I see her again. I think he's right. I call Judy.

It still surprises me when I hear other people, even my age and younger, talk about their lives, which so parallel my own. They aren't skaters, but they are sons and daughters, brothers, sisters, husbands and wives, whose lives are affected by someone else's alcoholism. I wish I'd known about this a long time ago. But then, I didn't even know Mom was an alcoholic or that it was an illness. I just thought she was ornery, mean, and hateful sometimes … and always when she drank. She's also a talented designer and seamstress who's wasted her life. I thought it was willful, and I thought she was lazy. Judy said it could be related to her husband's death; her way of mourning, or something. Sometimes I hated her for it. I'm tired of taking care of us. I was a kid; she was supposed to take care of me. Now Al-Anon is helping me sort out the pieces, even here, hundreds of miles away from the messed up puzzle of my home. I'm beginning to feel hopeful that when we put all these pieces together we'll see a beautiful picture emerge. I lie on my bed and fiddle with my good luck necklace. *Why isn't she answering the phone?*

I check my mailbox and carry the mail to my room. I open an Easter greeting. It's a yellow fuzzy chick pecking out of a colored egg. "Just popped out to say Happy Easter." It's signed, "Thinking about you. Happy birthday, Happy Easter, Love, Mom." I hold the card to my breast and the tears won't be checked. Mom hasn't remembered my birthday for, oh, so long. I'm not always sure myself, anymore, what the exact date is. We don't celebrate it, or talk about it. But maybe Mom, the new Sober Mom, is remembering the exact date of my birth. Perhaps she's remembering something joyful about it. I've only heard about the bad things in her life that all seem to coincide with my birth.

"Hi, Mom, how are you? I've tried several times to reach you, but I haven't found you in. You must have a really active social life these days." I laugh and I hear Mom laugh a little.

"I see you in the paper; congratulations, you're doing great. Yes, of course I read the papers."

"Thanks, Mom." I've never seen Mom read a newspaper. *Does she see the paparazzi too?* "Thanks for the birthday card, Mom."

"Sienna, I'm wondering about this. You don't have to agree, of course. You have your life, I have mine, I understand if you don't want this, okay, so don't worry and be honest, okay?"

"Yeah, sure. What it is?"

"I'm thinking I might like to take a bus trip to Colorado Springs and visit you there. I mean, I won't come if you don't want me to. But I checked on the bus schedule. I have a couple new designs to show you, and I'd sort of like to meet the Revue Producer in person. I mean, he's a good customer and all, and … well, good business, you know—

"Mom, stop! I'd love to have you come. Did you know I'll

be graduating from the baccalaureate program in three more weeks? It's a pretty big deal, you know, it's like regular high school graduation. I'll get a diploma. I've done really well in school, too. Would you like to come to that? And we have our big annual production just before that, and your costumes and—"

"I'll be there."

For the first time in my life, I believe she will actually be here. I pull the invitations out of my desk drawer. I only ordered two; I never dreamed I'd send either of them.

The Broadmoor Academic Program

Announces the Baccalaureate Program for the

Class of 1978

May 12, 1978

Scove Auditorium

2:00 pm

Conferring of Diplomas

Keynote Speaker, Peggy Fleming

I walk to the bus stop. It's a long walk, but I know we'll have to take a taxi to the hotel. Even though my school money account always has money in it, I'm terribly frugal, always afraid it might run out and I'll not get any more.

On my long walk to the bus and with my academic career about over, I think about that money: lessons, ice time, coach and trainer, school tuition, books, new skates every few months, skate maintenance, the required health insurance, board and room, travel expenses. *Where had all that money come from?*

She was so anxious to get rid of me, to send me here, I thought she'd pay anything to have me gone. But now, looking back ... kids don't always see the whole picture, and I certainly hadn't. Lessons aren't free. My education was expensive. My coach and trainer are the tops in their field. I don't even know how much skates cost because I've never paid for them. The money shows up in my school account magically, and my expenses are deducted automatically, I never pay, I never owe, I never see the balance. Whose money? I thought Mom and I were poor. We live in the poorest part of Tacoma. Mom's business is going great now, but what about all those years with no income? How does this money show up in accounting? I'm awash in gratitude, and sudden curiosity.

"Mom! Over here!" I jump up and down and watch the bus driver help her down the narrow metal steps of the bus. She hobbles my way. I hug her and she hugs me back, sort of, patting me on the shoulders. She feels smaller. She's lost some weight. But she's standing taller. She puts her hands on my face and kisses me on both cheeks – like Europeans do. *What was that?*

We walk to the side of the bus where the driver is
extracting suitcases from the bowels of the Greyhound. I step
inside the depot and order a cab. I get Mom settled at the
Woodrow Wilson Hotel. We walk as fast as I can move us past
the dining room and the bar in the hotel. I don't want her to
even know there is a bar. My stomach is convulsing. *Maybe
this visit isn't such a good idea.*

"You going to be okay, Mom? I have ice at four and then
I'll come back here and we can go to supper. Okay?" I give her
a quick kiss on the cheek and feel an undeniable compulsion to
get out of her room quickly before something happens.
Something always happens.

She reaches out and holds my shoulders. Then she kisses
me on each cheek. Again. Very tenderly. *Where did she get
that? This is too strange.* I had hurried in for ice at four, and
didn't linger as I came off. I quickly cover my blades, ready to
run to the locker room when Ziggy appears, smiling.

"Can I give you a lift?"

"Oh, thanks, Ziggy, but I'm headed downtown. Mom is
here for graduation and the ice revue. She's at the Woodrow
Wilson, and I'm meeting her for supper."

"Great! And how's that going?"

"So far, so good. The first thirty minutes, anyway." We
laugh. "I really am nervous, Ziggy."

"You'll be fine. She'll be fine. Come on, I'll drive you."

"You have a date tonight? Sorry, not my business. You

just look so nice, that's all. I don't usually see you with a neck tie and shined shoes. I don't mean to be nosy, but I really am curious."

"More like nosy." He grins. I know he isn't going to tell me.

Chapter Forty-Seven

When I get to Mom's room, she isn't quite ready to leave and is still in the bathroom. I change into a dinner dress. She has a mess of sketches and fabrics on her bed. I can see she's getting ready for her meeting tomorrow with the producer. I'm really proud of Mom for doing so well with her business. *But how long can this last?*

"These look great, Mom. What would you like to eat?" I call through the bathroom door.

"Actually, I hope you don't mind, but I took the liberty of making us a reservation at the *Silver Spur.*"

"You did? The Silver Spur?" *How on earth did she know about that place?* "I hear the food's okay, but it's really just a local hangout. It's a favorite date place, from what I hear. It's kind of a landmark, been here a long time, but I've never been there. Sure, we'll have us a date! Where did you hear about it?"

"Good! Okay, I'm almost ready." Mom floors me when she steps into the room.

"You look great, Mom. I like the hair cut." She looks fabulous wearing light makeup, looking so awake, so alert, and about ten years younger. She even has her nails done. She must have made her outfit. It fits too perfectly to be off the rack. Her figure is trim and she really looks terrific. I hardly know what to say, so, rudely, I just stare.

She smiles and gathers her purse and light jacket. I watch her limp and sway to the door and realize that she'd made one leg of her suit wider to fit over the brace. When she stands still, legs together, it looks like a long formal skirt. It's stunning. I've never seen her earrings before but the rubies sparkle and so do her eyes.

When we step out the front door, the doorman holds her elbow and steadies her down the steps to the street where a cab stands waiting. She looks so elegant. Like a princess, or a queen.

"Allow me?" A man steps out and takes mom's elbow and steers her past the taxi.

"Ziggy! What are you doing?"

"It's okay, Sienna. I've invited him to join us for dinner."

"Oh. Okay. I guess." *But I wanted some time alone with Mom.*

Ziggy tucks Mom into the back seat and I slide in beside her. Ziggy walks around the car to get into the front while I whisper into Mom's ear.

"I told you he was not my boyfriend. Why did you invite him?"

Ziggy slams the door and starts the car. My mom smiles smugly and winks at me. She winked at me! My mom has never winked at me. What in the world is happening? The Al-Anon didn't tell me what to do with New Sober Mom who runs a business, makes reservations, kisses cheeks, and winks.

"I see why the Silver Spur is a favorite date hang out. All the tables are so romantic and so private. You can't see anyone else, only your dinner partner. Nice, isn't it?" Mom looks over her shoulder suspiciously, like she thinks someone might be looking at her.

The food is so-so, but Mom and Ziggy enjoy their own laughter. I keep waiting for something to happen. Mom is a great spoiler. What will she do tonight to spoil this? It isn't over yet. I'm afraid to have too much fun, and my appetite is dull.

"Michael, didn't they used to have a Bird of Paradise mural painted on the wall next to this table?"

"Yes, I believe you're right. Actually, I seem to remember it was the Phoenix bird rising out of flame."

" That's right, now I remember. And they also have new silverware, notice that?"

"Oh, sure, I remember … they used to have spurs on the plastic handles. They've upgraded." They laugh like they're sharing a private joke, like old friends.

"How would you know that?" I ask it straight forward, not sarcastic, not snotty or anything. I can't say it with any emotion because at this moment, I have none. I am totally bewildered. "How? … have you?… been here before? When? Mom, have you been here before? I thought … only Tacoma …" I look from one to the other. They look perfectly relaxed and normal.

Mom looks … healthy, well. But me? *I'm confused.* My stomach convulses.

"I have been here. It was a long, long time ago. I'd like to tell you about that, Sienna. Would you like me to tell you about it?"

I look at Ziggy, my Al-Anon friend. *Should I agree to hear this story? Should I let her tell me? Is this going to turn into a disaster?*

"Why did Mom just call you Michael? Is that your real name?"

"I think you'll want to hear this story, Sienna. And, yes, my name really is Michael."

"You've been here, too? What is this, a little reunion or something? How do you—"

"Yes, it's a reunion; a long overdue reunion," he said. They reach across the table and hold each other's hands. I'm feeling very uncomfortable, and left out. Then they each take one of my hands.

"Think of it as a *family* reunion. Or a ride on a Zamboni," Mom jokes.

Ziggy laughs, then he looks at Mom; she stares him right in the eyes and they both smile.

"I've always wanted to ride on a Zamboni," I murmur suspiciously, with only a tad of sarcasm. I feel disaster coming on.

Chapter Forty-Eight

GINA

"I don't know where to begin, Sienna, Michael. I only want you both to know that I am so sorry to have screwed up so badly that I destroyed you along with myself. I want to do better. If you can forgive me, and be patient with me, I want to tell you how it all went so wrong.

"Michael is your father, Sienna. We were ... still are, actually, married." Sienna stares at Ziggy with one hand over her mouth. Michael bends to kiss her forehead as tears begin to fill her eyes. I feel so horrible for her. It's been so unfair. Michael wraps an arm around her and lays her head against his shoulder. Her tears stream. *He is such a good person. What a fool I am.*

"I never knew, Michael, never understood why you loved me. I still don't. I didn't love me; how could you? I thought you loved the skater. I only loved myself when I was on the ice. I didn't want you to know who I really was. The truth is I didn't really know who I was. I only knew I was a skater. Sienna, listen, because this is your story, too." I took a deep breath. Sienna sat up. I couldn't read the emotion in her eyes. *Does she hate me?*

I confess that I'm from a mafia family, and I tell them about the witness protection we are living under, and have been since Sienna was born. They both listen intently and respect my wish not to be interrupted or ask any questions until I finish. They both look pale when they hear what happened to my leg. Michael thought Marian had an accident on the ice, or in a car. Sienna imagined that I'd had polio. I tell her she's close.

"I died a little bit with my mama, Sienna. She was the one part of my identity that I did know, and that part died of polio. By the way, Sienna, your name is the home of your grandmother: Sienna, Italy. Another part of me died with my team in the plane crash. I've lived with the guilt of both.

"I believed that when I could no longer skate, I could no longer be loved. How could you love me? I thought I was doing the honorable thing by ending our marriage. I didn't know about Sienna yet. I never thought about how you would feel. I didn't get the love part at all, Michael. You deserve so much more. I never thought I was worthy of you, Sienna. I didn't know what to do with a baby. I was so young. I didn't know how to love a child any more than I knew how to love you, Michael.

"For the longest time, Sienna, I didn't understand that you were a gift from God. I thought you were my punishment from God for rushing into marriage, or for being part of a mafia family, or letting my mother die, or for not being on that plane. But now I see the truth. You are here to save me. Without you,

I would have ended my life sixteen years ago. The two of you ... the two of you ..." *Get a grip.* I swipe a tear and gasp for breath. "The two of you deserve so much more than me, what I was, what I still am. Now that you have each other, I feel better about that. But I'm not worthy of either of you."

They both start to butt in. I put my hands up. "Stop. I'm not finished."

I tell them about my life as Gina in a mafia family, and how I started drinking. They sit in stunned silence. As I talk, I begin to understand better myself, how alcohol had created a hiding place for me.

Sienna sniffs quietly. *This is a lot for her to take in.* Michael wipes his eyes. He hands Sienna a napkin and hugs her shoulders.

"Now you know everything." I have no more words.

"My life has been so empty without you." Michael speaks first. "Whether you believe it or not, Sienna and I are not leaving you. We are a family. We love you, Gina. And I'm so happy to have found you both. Love isn't about deserving. It's not about pay back. It's not something you can earn. It's about being. Right now, this minute. Let your heart be here, Gina."

Sienna wipes her nose and smiles a little. "So your name is really Gina? I like that, Mom."

At ten o'clock our waiter pokes his head around our screen and asks if we need anything else; the restaurant is closing. We pay our bill and leave.

"Pay attention to this, Sienna," I say, "and remember that classy people don't gyp, they tip." Sienna looks startled and puzzled. She watches as I stuff the bills under the salt and pepper.

"You're a big tipper, Mom." She must have many questions, but is probably so overwhelmed she can't say anything. We have so much to catch up with.

We go back to the hotel and the next four hours are unlike any Zamboni ride I have ever imagined. We press out several small cracks that are so insidious, so subtle, that most of the world would never know they're there. We polish the nicks and chinks that trip us, make us fall, make us angry, looking to get even. We skate deliberately over the wide dangerous cracks, where lesser skaters might fall and never recover. Back and forth we drive that Zamboni, telling, asking, crying, answering, until all the scary cracks began to close and heal. We're still fragile; we all know that. But for now, the surface is ready for a smoother skate into the empty arena that has been our life.

The lives we've been living are forever changed. No one knows what the future holds, not really. We can make plans, but only God knows what to do with them. We're all taking one day at a time. We're taking it slow. It's like learning new figures. We hold hands when it's slippery, and we'll drive the Zamboni whenever it gets rough. And it will.

"Mom, can you remember a time when you felt at peace? Like all was right in your world?"

I think about her question and search my heart for the most truthful answer I can give her.

"Yes. When I was a little girl, before my mother died, Sundays were special days for our family. My family was really only me, my mother, my uncle, the body guards, and then the assorted 'cousins.' But Sundays no one worked. We had a big dinner. We all went to Mass together. I sat between my mother and Uncle Giovanni. The entire congregation became my family as we knelt and prayed together. It was a safe, reassuring feeling. Yes, like all was right in my world."

"Then, that's what we have to go back to, Mom. That's what we have to do."

"Oh, Sienna, I'm so sorry. You should have had that all your life. It's my fault that ..."

"Stop, Mom. The apologies have all been said, all the way around. Now it's time to put ourselves back together."

"Sienna's a smart girl, isn't she, Gina?"

I smile. "Yes, she certainly is. Like her father, I'd say." Michael pulls a silly humble face.

"Then that's what we'll do from now on. Sundays will be special. Church, dinner, safe, reassuring Sundays. Okay with you guys?" Sienna's eyes gleam hopeful.

Michael and I both grin like the kids we used to be and wrap our arms around each other. "Okay with us."

We go to church, AA, Al-Anon, and live prayerfully, one day at a time. I've quit looking over my shoulder and we've opened the drapes. I've accepted that God does love me, and I've learned to love in return. We skate through our lives' programs giving it our best shot, our all: concentration, energy, enthusiasm, work, and devotion. We're taking one day at a time. The life I had so carefully planned wasn't the life God had planned for me. Now we go where God leads us.

I finally am in charge of my life. By turning my life over to God, I'm finally in charge of me.

AUTHOR'S NOTE

This is a work of fiction. Some of the incidents are historical fact, and many of the names in the story were and are real people, though the main characters are fictional. Most of the story of the mafia is based on fact, though not necessarily chronologically accurate. The ice skating history is factual and the plane crash, sadly, was real.

Polio: Before your time, dear Readers, parents lived in fear of summer polio epidemics. Children were warned to take naps every day, were not allowed in public swimming pools, and forbidden to eat peaches with fuzz, which they feared might carry the virus. Kids were even kept out of church and Sunday school. No one really understood why this horrible epidemic attacked in the summer. In 1952, there were 57,879 cases. The monstrous iron lung in the parlor was greatly feared. The Salk vaccine was tested in 1954 and found to be safe and effective. Lucky you!

Wyandotte, Michigan: The Detroit mafia based in southeastern Michigan and Toledo, Ohio, had its epicenter in Wyandotte in an area known as Little Sicily.

Chicago Piano: the "official" nickname of the submachine gun favored by organized crime.

Broadmoor Skating Club: In its sixty-year history, the

Broadmoor Skating Club has had eight members medal at the Olympics. Three of them won gold, and over 200 nationalists call Broadmoor home. The club hosted the World Championships in 1957 and 1959, and the Nationals in 1961. The Broadmoor later changed its name to The World Arena Ice Hall. In 2009, it became known as Colorado Gold.

Smoking: In the 1950s, '60s, and even into the early '70s, smoking was very common among athletes. It was glamorized. The commercial breaks on the CBS "Sunday Sports Spectacular" and the broadcast of the National Figure Skating Championships featured the top figure skaters smoking and advertising the sponsors' brands. The broadcasters and announcers themselves smoked while on the air. They didn't know what you know now. Today's athletes know better.

Al-Anon: This is a very real and free organization. If someone you know or care about, a friend or family member, suffers from the disease of alcoholism, you need some help. If drinking is a way of life for you, please call Ala-Teen. Find it on the web at http//:www.al-anon.alateen.org/for-alateen. Call 1-888-4AL-ANON (1-888-425-2666). Your local newspaper will most likely list a contact locally. Don't wait, dear Readers. Call them today. You are loved.

DISCUSSION QUESTIONS

1. Gina has her mind set on winning Olympic Gold. Was this a realistic goal for her? Is it a realistic goal for most athletes? What are some characteristics necessary for performance athletes?

2. Have you ever suffered a disappointment so great you thought you'd never get over it? How were you able to cope and move on?

3. Why do you think Gina wasn't able to do that? What was missing for her?

4. What is your opinion of Salvatore Giovanni?

5. What *could* have happened that would have changed how Gina lived her life?

6. In what ways was Sienna like Gina? In what ways was she different?

7. What role do you think Sienna played in Gina's recovery?

8. How would you write the next chapter in the life of Gina, Michael, and Sienna?

9. What is one message you will remember from Gina's story?

RESOURCES

Al-anon, From Survival to Recovery: Growing up in an Alcoholic Home; Al-anon Family Groups.

Broadmoor Skating Club History: www.broadmoorsc.com/History

Lunde, Paul. *Organized Crime.*

Detroit Partnership. Wikipedia. Web.

Loosemore, Sandra. *Retrospective: 1961 US Figure Skating Championships.* Aug 2000. Web.

Machi, Mario. *Detroit Crime Bosses.*

Smith, Beverly. *A Year in Figure Skating.* McLelland & Stewart.

Smith, Beverly. *Figure Skating, A Celebration.* McLelland & Stewart. 1994.

World Figure Skating Museum & Hall of Fame, Colorado Springs, Colorado. Karen Cover, Administrative Coordinator.

ACKNOWLEDGEMENTS

I sincerely thank Kathie Blozan, Cashiers, NC, Sharon Harris, Brevard, NC, Bob and Ellie Kassem, Knoxville, TN, for sharing important background information for my story.

Thank you to Karen Cover, Colorado Springs, CO, for archival research at the Ice Skating Hall of Fame and Museum.

To the Royal Scribblers of Cashiers, NC, Joy Neaves, Smoky Mountain Writing Group at UNCA for comments and suggestions; thank you all.

To Chris Godsey, Dr. Sandra Hartman, and Debby Lazoff, my heartfelt thanks for early readings and encouragement.

Thank you to Brooke Batchelor for a first read from a Y/A perspective.

And always, a thanks to my patient husband, my live-in IT guy. The computer and I couldn't do this without your help.

Thanks to Tracy Ruckman for her editorial skills and Write Integrity Press for their trust, and for loving Gina.

Thanks to all of you.

Look for other books

published by

www.WriteIntegrity.com

and

Pix-N-Pens Publishing

www.PixNPens.com